WH(
WC

THE FIRST IN THE
PARALLEL UNIVERSE
ADVENTURES

PAM BLOOM

Whole New World[s]
Copyright © Pam Bloom

Published by Pam Bloom Publishing

ISBN: 978-0-9955272-1-8

Cover design by Ilan Sheady,
www.ilanimationstudios.com

Author's note: This book was written and
produced in the UK, and uses British
English language conventions.

For my dad, Bernard Bloom,
Without whom I would literally not be here.
Nor literally!

Connect with the author at
www.pambloomauthor.com -

Sign up for Pam's email list
and you will be sent FREE scifi reads

Don't miss out!

Great life, huh?

Have you ever wanted to be somewhere else? Or to be *someone* else? I bet you have. I mean, it's not as if your life is perfect, right? No-one's is.

Before last summer, I'd often wanted to give up my life – even just for a day – and live somewhere else, in someone else's body, doing different, less boring, things. Maybe riding a flash car, or a speedboat, or a motorbike – yeah, a motorbike would be good. Being free to speed along the road, not a care in the world, able to go anywhere, do anything. Wouldn't it be great?

...Yeah, right. Back in the real world, I was too young to ride a bike even if I could afford one. Even a pushbike was beyond me, and being an 11-year-old boy with a sick mother and an annoying little sister was beginning to get on my nerves.

Before the events of last summer, I was stuck in an

old, painfully dull routine, which mainly consisted of, as mum put it, 'being the man of the house.'

This mainly meant getting up early, seeing to mum and Lizzie, walking to school, hating school, being bullied at lunchtime, hating school some more, trying to get out of school without bumping into Sean Roberts, going home, getting tea ready, doing homework if I could be bothered, watching TV with Lizzie, making her do *her* homework (which is more important), sending her to bed then, finally, after what seemed like an eternity of boredom, falling into bed myself.

Great life, huh?

Actually, it was – but, as with most things, I didn't appreciate it at the time.

And then something happened in the summer which changed everything. My whole life was turned upside-down. No, that's too simple – my whole understanding of the *universe* was turned upside-down and, more importantly, I came to realise that my life wasn't as bad as I had thought it was.

I don't suppose you'll believe me when I tell you the details, but that doesn't matter. I have to tell someone.

My name is Ethan. Ethan Jones.

It all began in August. We had broken up for the summer holidays, and I had been feeling pretty happy, as I always do at the prospect of six long weeks without school. Six long weeks without homework I didn't have time to do. Six long weeks without having to get up at six o'clock every weekday to see to mum and Lizzie before the long walk to school. Six blissful weeks without the name-calling. Six ecstatic, fantastic weeks without Sean Roberts.

It was a couple of weeks into the holidays, when I was just beginning to get a bit bored, that it happened.

Sorry, I'm getting ahead of myself. I forget you don't know me. Not yet. I'd better tell you a bit about myself first, hadn't I?

I was 11. Just – my birthday's in August, which means I've always been one of the youngest in my class. Which may just explain why I've always felt

7

like I didn't belong, why I was useless at everything. Why I was always way behind everyone else.

I suppose I first noticed it when I was about five – you know, when school starts getting serious and you stop just playing around in the sand pit. Reading, writing, maths – I was rubbish at all of them. Still am. Hate reading. Can't see the point of it. We have films and TV, why do we need to read? And maths? What's *that* all about? I told Mrs Perkins – she was my maths teacher – we have calculators now, why do I need to know what eight sixes are? She wasn't too pleased. Made me recite my six and eight times tables in front of the whole class. Twice.

I was about six or seven when the other kids noticed I was different. If you're not the same as them they pick on you. It doesn't matter if it's because you're clever or thick, too skinny or too fat, a different colour or have a strange accent, they soon notice and take the mickey. Most of them stop after a while. Others enjoy it enough to make your life a misery for the rest of your school life.

With me it wasn't being thick – I'm not stupid, just not interested – but my home life that made me different. My mum's ill – she's got something called ME, or Chronic Fatigue Syndrome. There's no cure, and apparently some doctors don't even believe it's an illness, so it's pretty drastic. Basically it means she can barely get out of bed most of the time.

When she's bad – we call it having an episode – she'll stay in bed for weeks without doing more than getting up to go to the toilet. So I have to make her meals, which she hardly touches, and bring her a bowl of hot water and a towel once a day so she can have a wash.

She's been like that for nearly as long as I can remember, though I know it's only since my dad left home when I was seven. Some people say it was dad leaving that made her ill. I don't know about that, I just know when dad left I stopped being her little boy and ended up being the man of the house.

And then there's Lizzie, of course. She's my little sister, and I've been looking after her, too, since dad left. She's eight this year, so she does a lot for herself now, but I still have to get her meals most of the time and iron her school clothes for her – she'd burn herself if I let her near the iron.

She's really clumsy. I remember once about a year ago I let her make her own tea and she burnt her hand on the cooker. She's still got a scar. I'll never forgive myself for that one. We were in casualty for *hours*.

So the kids at school noticed I never went to their parties, never invited them back home. How could I? If anyone found out how bad mum was they would have taken us away from her – that's what mum said, and she was right.

School was bad enough before I started being bullied. Afterwards it became a nightmare, but I couldn't skive off too often – if I started doing that the teachers would notice, and send the social workers round to the house. So I had to put up with Sean Roberts and his gang of idiots stealing my books, hiding my gym kit, flinging my shoes over the fence and throwing things at me in class when the teacher's back was turned.

I couldn't even fight back to make them stop, because if I did the teachers would want to come round and see my mum. As it is I had to make excuses every time they wanted her to go to school for parent's evenings and that. They just thought she was a bad mother, that she didn't care enough to turn up.

Thank goodness for Jake. If it wasn't for him, I think I would have run away long ago.

Jake is my best friend – my only friend, really – and he's just brilliant. He's so clever he makes Stephen Hawkins look dumb. Once he told Mr Thompson – he was our science teacher – how some theory or other works, and made him literally speechless. I've never seen anyone drop their jaw in astonishment before, unless they were doing it as a joke, that is, but Thommo stood there open-mouthed for about a minute while the whole class fell about laughing.

Later, when the rest of the class had left, Jake apologised to Mr Thompson, who looked even more embarrassed than before and muttered something about Einstein which I didn't understand. Jake's like that, you see. He's really clever but nice with it, and he knows everything about my family without me having to tell him. He just knows.

Anyway, I can't blather on about myself all day, I've got an adventure to tell you about. And what an adventure it was.

The coastguard house

It was a Friday in the middle of August, and I'd had a bad week. The weather had been rubbish, which meant staying in a lot, and mum had been less energetic than normal. I'm not sure why, but she always seems worse when we're off school.

Maybe it's the pressure of having us around all day – I don't know – but it was the fourth day of her staying in bed and I was sick of looking after her. I mean, I love her of course, but sometimes I get tired of being the adult in the relationship.

So after I'd made her and Lizzie some lunch and cleaned up afterwards, I decided to go for a walk to get away from it all for a bit. Mum was in bed – again – and Lizzie was watching TV.

I have this place I go to, down on the waterfront. We live about half a mile from the sea, on the edge of a little village with one shop, one bus stop and one pedestrian crossing. Seriously, it's that exciting. There's so little to do here it's unbelievable – the nearest proper shops are two miles away, and me and Lizzie have to walk a mile to school; it takes us about half an hour. In the winter that's hell, especially with Lizzie stopping every five minutes to stroke a cat or pick up a leaf.

Anyway, our house is an old detached one in its own gardens, surrounded by a big wall. Mum has lived in it since she was a little girl, as her mum and dad bought it years ago. It sounds posh, but it's really not. Yeah, we have lots of room, but the place is falling apart – I have to do all the repairs, as we haven't got any money, and I'm not really that good at decorating yet. Downstairs is a bit damp, and it can smell when the weather's wet, which is most of the time where we live!

So when I'm fed up I have to get out, and I always head towards the sea. I like the space, the sky stretching away into the distance, the crunch of sand under my feet as I walk up the beach. There's not much to do there – sometimes I collect things that have washed up with the tide, sometimes I fish a little off the old jetty, though there's never anything to catch. At other times I just walk and walk and walk until my feet are sore and I have to turn back before it goes dark.

On this particular day the weather had brightened up a bit and the sun was actually trying to peek through the clouds, so it was a pleasant walk along the dirt footpath that leads through the dunes to the beach. You hardly ever see anyone else down there – that's one of the reasons I like it, I suppose – maybe a dog walker or two, occasionally a bird spotter, but today I was alone.

I trudged down the beach towards the island, which is cut off from the mainland most of the day by the tide, and started humming a tune to myself. As I drew level with the only building down there, the old coastguard house, which has been empty for years, I noticed something odd. One of the boards over the windows had been taken off.

Now, I walk on the beach a lot in the summer, maybe three times a week, and so I know every square inch of the area. I know where the gullies are and when they are going to be full; I know how to walk round the sewage outlet without having to get your feet muddy; I know when a tree has fallen down in the wind. So it was a big surprise to see the hole in the window space.

I walked over to investigate. The coastguard house is a small, one-storey brick building just off the beach, with a little wall in front and a yard behind. It was decommissioned about ten years ago, I think, and has been empty ever since. Why they didn't knock it down I don't know – it's been slowly falling down itself over the years.

It was clear the board had been taken off, rather than fallen off, as it had been placed neatly to one side. I peered in through the window – miraculously, the glass was still intact – and saw a dusty, nearly empty room with bare floorboards and a dirty fireplace.

There was nothing in there except a few bits of

16

paper lying on the floor and a crumpled cigarette packet on the mantelpiece. Then something caught my eye. Through the open door to the room I could see daylight, which was odd because I knew from previous exploring that the whole house was boarded up. Obviously someone had removed a board at the back of the house as well, because light was now streaming through.

Pleased to have something to do other than walk and think, I went round to the back of the house, crunching on broken glass and bits of old wood, pushing my way through nettles and gorse bushes. A few scratches later I came to the yard, which I knew from previous visits contained nothing worth looking at, and headed to the back door. Then I stopped dead. The door was open.

Wow. This was big. Somebody had been here. Not only been here, but been breaking into the old house. That in itself didn't bother me, of course – I didn't care if a tramp moved in; they could bring their whole family, if they liked, it was no skin off my nose – no, what I was worried about was if they were still there. I didn't want to walk into a teenager's drug den or be beaten up by a drunken old biddy.

I decided to approach more stealthily, creeping up to the side of the door before looking in. Directly inside was the old kitchen, with a disused cooker and grimy old sink. Whoever had been here clearly wasn't using the kitchen to make spaghetti Bolognese, anyway.

Slowly I stepped over the threshold and into the kitchen, listening intently for any sign of life. Maybe someone had just been here for a couple of days before moving on, or perhaps some kids had decided to use it as a playhouse? Nah, no kid could have got that board off the front, it had been nailed on, and the back door looked like it had been forced open. This had to be the work of an adult.

The thought made me nervous as I slowly edged further into the house. What would I do if someone objected to me being here? Run like hell, I supposed. Whatever, I walked slowly further into the kitchen.

It smelt a bit musty, but not too bad – I suppose the back door being open had let in some fresh air. There was grime and dirt everywhere, mice droppings on the floor and dust in the air, but I could tell with a bit of cleaning up this place might actually still be habitable.

Leading off from the kitchen was a small corridor, and I peered into this slowly, my heart beating in my chest so hard I thought I could actually hear it. There was nothing – and no-one – there, so I walked a little further inside, noticing the bare carpet and old information posters on the wall.

The corridor led to the front room, which I had looked into before, so I already knew no-one was there. There was a toilet, which I could see into, plus another room off, which I peered into cautiously. Inside was another small fireplace, a threadbare and very dirty rug, and a sleeping bag lying next to a portable stove – you know, the sort you take on camping trips – with dirty pans and empty tins of beans and hot dogs lying around it.

A couple of empty Coke cans lay strewn across the

rug, and there was a broken mug on top of the mantelpiece.

OK, I thought, someone's been sleeping here, using this place as a temporary hideaway. There was no-one here now, anyway... although they could come back any minute. This thought made me uneasy, and I was about to leave when I saw something shining on the floor next to the sleeping bag. This was strange, as it was pretty gloomy in here and no direct light as far as I could see to make something shine.

I quickly walked into the room, noticing as I did some dirty clothes piled in one corner, and bits of odds and ends seemingly just flung to one side – my mind took in a bent fork, a box of matches, an old newspaper and a single woollen glove. Hastily, I bent down and picked the shining thing up.

Straight away, the room went black, and all was oblivion.

A path to pigs

I opened my eyes slowly. The light hurt them.

I was still standing in the room at the old coastguard house. I shook my head to clear it and a dizzy spell washed over me, so I crouched down until I felt normal again.

What *was* that? It seemed like I'd blacked out for a second or two, but I had remained standing, so that was weird. I thought when you fainted you usually fell down.

Whatever it was seemed to have passed, anyway, so I stood up again and looked about me. I had to get out of here before the squatter came back.

I still had the shining thing in my hand, and I looked at it briefly. It was silver, about the size of a two pound coin, oval in shape and slightly flatter on one side than the other, like an egg that has been squashed. Smooth on the surface, it seemed to be

21

made out of metal, and was pretty heavy, like a pebble off the beach, but it looked odd. You know that silver hologramatic wrapping paper which reflects the colours of the rainbow? It was a bit like that, and seemed to give off a faint shine, like an old glow stick that's losing its power – although maybe that was my imagination.

I put it deep in my front jeans pocket and walked out of the house.

Outside, the sun was shining a lot brighter than when I had gone in. I looked at the sky and was mildly surprised to see no clouds at all.

Deciding I'd had enough excitement for one day, I turned left along the beach and headed for the pathway back to the village. The sand was shining in the sun, and seemed to have an oddly orange tinge, as it sometimes does when the sun is setting over the water. Odd. I looked up at the sky, and was more than a little disturbed to see it, too, appeared a different colour to normal – a darker blue than it usually is.

Putting this down to the 'blackout' I had

22

experienced in the deserted house – maybe it had affected my vision – I carried on. I certainly *felt* normal.

I reached the path and turned down it – and immediately stopped dead.

Hang on. This wasn't right.

The pathway, which I had walked along hundreds of times, was different.

Sure, it was in the same place as normal, and it went in the same direction, but its surface was now gravel, not just ground – or, more accurately most of the year, mud.

Someone from the council must have come along and put gravel on the path while I was on the beach. But how was that possible? Surely I'd only arrived here less than an hour ago?

I looked at my watch, and was shocked to discover it said half past four. Half past four! I'd left the house after lunch, about one o'clock, and it only takes 15 minutes or so to get down to the beach, and another five-ish to reach the coastguard house. So where had the time gone?

I crunched down the path, mind in a whirl, and noticed another odd thing. If this gravel had only just been laid down – which, logically, it must have been – why did it not look fresh? Muddy and sandy almost all over, it had footprints, leaves, and, even worse, small weeds growing up in places.

This was beginning to worry me. Perhaps that blackout had affected me more than I'd realised. Maybe I had had some sort of seizure or something. Maybe I was even going mad, and the path had always been gravel.

I was just mulling this thought over when I saw something that convinced me: I *was* mad.

Coming along the path towards me was Mrs Powell, an old lady from the village who used to work in the school as a dinner lady before she retired. I often saw her out walking her dog, Bertie, a King Charles spaniel, and she always said hello and sometimes stopped to have a chat about the weather and ask how mum was. She was a nice old dear, and usually I was glad to see her. Not today.

Today, although she looked the same, and was wearing the same battered raincoat she always wore, rain or shine, she didn't have Bertie on the lead she was holding. Oh no, that would have been too normal on an afternoon that was rapidly turning into the strangest one I'd ever had. No, today she was walking a pig.

I stopped dead as she walked past me, seemingly not recognising me although we'd met hundreds of times. The pig was a big beast, one of those hairy pink ones with big black spots. Its snout was covered in mud and it had a blue collar round its neck, with a little tag on, presumably for its name and address. Its trotters dug into the gravel as it passed me by, and it snuffled at my leg when it went past, leaving a muddy patch on the denim.

I shut my eyes, hoping this would all go away. The sand, the sky, the path – and now this. It was all too much. Suddenly I just wanted to be at home, in my bedroom, watching boring telly and deciding what to make for tea. I wanted to feel normal again.

I started running along the path, my trainers flinging up the gravel which by rights shouldn't be there, my heart beating faster.

When I came to the end of the path I didn't slow down but raced along the main street, feet making a slapping noise on the pavement. At least *that* seemed normal, down to the dried up chewing gum dotted here and there. I'd half expected it to have turned to gold.

As I ran past the bus stop I saw a poster on the wall which hadn't been there before. I think it was advertising a play or something, but I didn't look at it properly.

I slowed down as I got to the shop, as I was running out of breath – but what I saw there made me stop completely, open-mouthed. Now I knew how Thommo had felt when Jake had shocked him in class. No, I felt worse than that. I felt like the whole world had changed while I'd been at the beach.

The shop was in the same place, but it wasn't the

26

usual one I visited almost daily. Instead of a large, plate-glass window covered in posters for lost dogs, old sofas for sale and the local amateur dramatics society's latest production, it had a battered metal shutter covering the whole of the front. A dirty grey colour, this was decorated with untidy graffiti which had obviously been scrawled by some idiot or other – odd squiggles, smiley faces and doodles which meant nothing covered its surface. The word 'SCUM' was painted in big, yellow letters close to the door.

I shut my mouth, and peered inside. Through the gloom, I could see that inside was just as bad. All the counters – holding the chocolate bars, newspapers, loaves of bread, even the chewing gum – were protected by those see-through plastic barriers. You may have seen them in sweet shops in the poorest council estates, where the local customers can't even be trusted to stand next to a Mars bar without stealing it.

They have small openings at the bottom next to the till so the staff can hand over the goods while you pay.

This wasn't the shop I knew. This wasn't the place at all. What on earth was going on?

I was rooted to the spot, not knowing what to do, when something bumped into my legs from behind. I turned to see – and I know you're not going to believe this – another pig, just like the one Mrs Powell had been walking before. This one was a bit smaller, and cleaner, but it was still a pig. It had a glittery pink collar round its hairy neck, attached to which was a brown leather lead.

The man holding the lead was carrying a plastic bag full of shopping, and struggling to control the pig, which started to sniff at my shoes. I recognised him as Mr Hughes, one of our neighbours. He had been a postman before he retired, and lived alone since his wife died last year. I often saw him out and about, doing his garden, walking to the shop for the paper, and he always said hello. I'd never seen him with a pig before.

"I'm so sorry, son," he said now, pulling the pig back. "Heel, Sammy."

I just stared at him, dumbstruck. He didn't seem to notice.

"It's OK," he said, "she won't bite."

He dragged the unwilling animal away from my feet and made it sit by pushing on its back end. He then proceeded to tickle it under the chin and scratch its ears.

"She's only a baby, aren't you, Sammy? We only got her two months ago – it was the wife's idea. She's not fully trained yet... the pig, that is, not the wife," he said, chuckling at his own joke, and making clucking noises to the pig as he scratched its floppy pink ears. The pig seemed to be enjoying itself. I certainly wasn't.

I wanted to ask him questions, to find out what was going on here, but I didn't know where to start – the path, the shop... the pigs?! Hang on, did he say getting the pig was his wife's idea? I thought she was dead!

I opened my mouth to speak, but only a little squeaking noise came out. I realised I didn't know what to say.

He stopped scratching the pig, and a puzzled look came over his face.

"Are you OK, son?" he asked.

I shook my head, not trusting my voice, and he peered at me through his glasses, his eyes narrowing as if he was trying to focus. What he said next made a shiver race down my spine and the hairs stick up at the back of my neck.

"I'm sorry, son, I don't know your name. Are you new round here?"

Nothing makes sense

That was it. I couldn't take this anymore.

Here, on top of everything else, was a man I had known since I was a toddler, out walking a pig on a lead, speaking of a wife I knew he no longer had, and denying he knew me. I saw him almost daily! Either *he* was going mad, or I was.

Managing to mumble something about being a stranger in town – which I certainly felt like at the time – I turned and fled down the road, leaving a puzzled Mr Hughes tying his pig's lead to a post outside the shop.

I couldn't stand any more of this madness. I had to get home, to mum and her moaning, to Lizzie and her annoying games. To my wonderful, peaceful, *normal* bedroom.

It didn't occur to me, then, that my home may be unrecognisable, too... but when I rounded the corner into my road, I started to get a feeling this wasn't going to end well. Slowing down, I walked up the street, eyes nearly popping out of my head.

Every house – so familiar, so often walked past – was slightly... well, *not right* is the best way to describe it. They all looked more or less the same as usual – a normal street of fairly affluent, semi-detached and detached homes – but I kept seeing things I'd never noticed before. No – which had never *been* there before.

There was a big oak tree in number 3's garden. The gate to number 7 was one of those fancy cast iron ones with spikes on top. Number 13 had a large sign saying 'No Hawkers' nailed to the porch. On the other side, number 12 was painted a bright green and had those intricate leaded windows which look like they take ages to clean. Next door's drive was covered in that white, gravelly stuff that spills out everywhere and cats use as litter trays. None of that was right. I didn't remember any of them.

And, to top it all, standing outside every house,

waiting to be emptied, stood a mustard yellow wheely bin. I could have sworn ours were green.

I nearly stopped there and then. Dreading what I'd see when I got to our house, I could easily have turned and carried on running until I got to Dover. I was that scared.

But – and here's the thing – I had nowhere else to go. If everything had changed, that meant nowhere was safe. And if all this was something to do with me having a blackout – maybe I was ill, and needed to go to hospital – then I needed to get home, fast. I had to find out. I had to go home.

I almost crept up past number 21, next door to ours. That, at least, seemed normal. The wall surrounding our house was still there, I was glad to notice, and there was still a big metal number 23 on the gate post. Maybe everything would be OK after all.

Barely daring to breathe, I walked in through the gate... and stopped dead for the umpteenth time that fateful afternoon.

33

I must have looked like I'd seen a ghost, I just stood there staring. Oh, the house was the same – sort of. It was the same building, you could see that, but it was totally different in so many ways.

The outside, instead of being plain red brick, had been coated with that sickly pinkish pebble dash stuff that never comes off. The windows were that tacky pvc that is supposed to look like wood but doesn't – ours (I mean to say, in the world I remembered; the world that made sense) were the original, old sash windows made of real wood, which is why the house is so draughty.

The garden, so untidy and wild in *my* world, was as neat as a stately home's grounds. There were manicured lawns on both sides of the house and box hedges running along either side of the drive. To one side of the house was a conservatory I'd never seen before.

But perhaps the biggest shock of all was the large black Mercedes car sitting on the driveway. Mum didn't drive, and we never had visitors.

I was suddenly in a total panic. This wasn't my house! What was I saying – this wasn't my *world*!

Quite aware it was a stupid and futile move, but not knowing what else to do, I fumbled in my jeans pocket for my door key. I took it out and looked at it. Hanging from a motorbike keyring I'd got as a birthday present from Jake one year, it looked same, thank goodness. At least something hadn't changed.

Glancing nervously around, I walked up to the door. This, too, was different. It was brown pvc, like the windows, and had a fake brass handle and letterbox. The key wasn't going to fit, I knew – how could it, it wasn't even the same door – but I tried it anyway, unaware at that point that I had started to cry, tears spilling down my cheeks and onto my t-shirt.

The key wouldn't even go in the lock. Hands shaking, I turned it over and tried again. And again.

Suddenly I heard a muffled voice coming from inside. It was a man. He sounded annoyed.

"Heather, I think there's someone at the door. Get

it, will you?" Heather is my mum's name.

Not knowing what to do, but having no intention of being found trying effectively to break into my own house, I dashed round the side and hid behind a large water butt that had mysteriously appeared at the corner. From here I could peer through a gap and see the front of the house.

I heard the door opening. There was a pause, and then it shut again. No-one came out.

I couldn't see anything from where I was, and although I wasn't sure I wanted to, I felt I had to see more of what was inside. Was my mum OK? Had she noticed everything changing, too? Who was the man? Maybe he had something to do with it?

Taking a deep breath, I turned and shuffled on my haunches towards the side window, my mum's bedroom window. Back when everything made sense, we had moved my mum's bedroom to the ground floor – we had plenty of space – so it would be easier for her to get around when me and Lizzie were at school. She liked having her bedroom here, because she could look out at the garden and watch the birds and squirrels. We put her bed right up against the window so she could easily see outside.

I reached the window, just having time to notice a side gate that had not been there that morning, and listened intently. Hearing nothing but my scared breathing, I decided to risk it and take a look. Gradually, I straightened up and peered in.

I immediately wished I hadn't. My mum's bedroom was not a bedroom any longer. It had been turned into a dining room, decorated with flowery wallpaper, with a neat wooden table and six chairs standing directly in the middle of the room. There was a bookshelf on one side, and one of those fancy dressers on the other, complete with plates and china ornaments. On top of the bookshelf were a couple of framed photos of people I didn't recognise, and there was a fake crystal chandelier hanging from the ceiling.

Nothing – nothing – was the same.

I sat down on the floor with a bump, back against

the cold pebble-dashed wall, feet outstretched, and started to sob. What on earth was going on? Ever since I'd blacked out in the old coastguard house, the world had gone mad. What should I do? Where could I go?

I realised I still had the useless door key in my hand, so I struggled to put it back in my front pocket. I may never need it again, but I wanted to hang on to familiar things right now.

As I was putting it away, I felt something hard and round in my pocket, and immediately remembered the metal pebble thing I'd found in the abandoned house. Carefully, I took it out and held it in the palm of my hand.

Drying my wet cheeks with the back of my hand, I looked at it more closely, turning it over slowly so I could examine its surface. It was truly strange. Although obviously metallic, it felt not only smooth but oddly soft, as if it was made of that suede-like material you sometimes find on cheap plastic animal toys. It was still giving off a silvery glow, although the sun was round the other side of the house and not shining on me at all. When I looked closely, I could see all the colours of the rainbow reflected on its surface.

As I looked, transfixed, I heard the front door opening again and the sound of voices, one raised, as someone came out of the house. I had to see. Turning once more, I hurried to hide behind the water butt again, from where I could peer through the gap between it and the wall. I could just see the car. A man standing with his back to me had his hand on the door handle. He was talking – well, shouting more accurately describes it.

"And tell that useless boy if he's late home again he'll have me to answer to. I want to know exactly what time he gets in. Did you hear me, Heather?"

The woman he was talking to came into view, carrying a briefcase. She looked a bit like my mum – but she, too, wasn't the same. My mum is painfully thin, while this woman was rather plump; her hair was tied in a neat bun, dyed brown with blonde streaks, while my mum's unkempt, greying hair hasn't been near a hairdresser's for years; and she was wearing a green, flowery dress and high-heeled shoes. My mum – wherever she was – only owned one dress and was always seen, on the rare times she went out of the house, in jeans and flat shoes.

I goggled at her. Who was she? Although in many ways familiar, she didn't even *sound* like my mum. Maybe she was an aunty I didn't know about? But why would she be called Heather, too? This was beginning to hurt my brain.

"Of course," she said, handing the man the briefcase. He opened the car door. "I'll be home at seven," he said. "Make sure my dinner's on the table when I get in. And none of that foreign muck like last night. It tasted like dogswill. I want a proper English dinner."

So saying, he turned to get into the car, and I saw his face for the first time. And this time I think my heart *did* stop.

It was my dad.

Home again

He was older, I could see that, but it was definitely my dad. Although I hadn't seen him for nearly four years, since he walked out on us, I would have known that face anywhere – mum didn't know this, but I had a photo of him, me and Lizzie taken the year before he left, hidden in my 'treasures' box, and I'd take it out sometimes and gaze at it, wondering why he left and if I'd ever see him again. Well, now I could see him.

His hair was a bit thinner and greyer than in that photo, and he had a small, neat beard, but his blue eyes and large, crooked nose – I remember he told me it had got broken in a fight when he was a teenager – were unchanged. He'd put on a couple of stone, too, by the looks of things. He was wearing what looked like an expensive grey suit – I remembered my dad wearing jeans all the time. Back before he left us, he was a plumber. I had no idea what he was now.

He got into the car, slammed the door shut and started the engine. Part of me wanted to dash out of my hiding place and run to him, to have him hug me again, but the larger part of me decided this would not be a good idea. Nothing here made sense, and I wanted to find out what was happening before I talked to anyone else.

So I watched him reverse the car out into the street and drive away, a pang of loss hitting me like heartburn. The woman – I refused to believe it was my mum – went back into the house, and I returned to my sitting position on the floor.

Rubbing my eyes, I tried to clear my head and think, like Jake would.

Jake! Maybe he'd know what was going on!

I reached into my back pocket and pulled out my mobile. It was an old model and a bit battered, but I was proud of it, anyway – I'd had to save up for months to buy it, and it was the only bit of high tech stuff I owned. Unlike most of the people in my school, I didn't have all the latest computers and games consoles – although we were lucky enough not to have a mortgage, mum was on benefits, so we could barely afford to feed and clothe ourselves, let alone buy luxuries.

I only spent a few pounds topping up the phone every month – usually texting Jake – so I knew I still had plenty of credit left.

I turned the phone over and looked at the screen. It was blank.

Thinking it must have switched itself off in my pocket, I pressed the on/off button and waited for it to spring into life. It stayed blank. Great, now my phone was broken. I put it back in my pocket, and turned once more to the 'stone' I'd found in the coastguard house.

Staring at it, I became more and more convinced that it was somehow the cause of all this. As far as I could remember, it was the act of picking it up off the floor that had caused me to black out – and from there, everything had gone weird.

Tentatively, as if it might explode at any moment,

I put it down on the tarmac in front of me. Slowly, I picked it up again. Nothing happened.

I turned it over in my hand, holding it close to my eyes so I could see every detail on its surface. It seemed flawless, completely smooth and – hang on, there was a thin indentation on one side, the rounder side. If I ran my finger ever so gently over it, I could just feel a slight change in its shape, going round in a circle, like a thin, hidden, button.

Not knowing what else to do, I put my finger on the middle of this 'button,' and pressed it.

All at once the world went black, just like before.

When I opened my eyes, it was to a dimmer world. My head hurt, and my back was aching. I looked to my right, and was not a little astonished to find the water butt, behind which I had so recently been hiding, had disappeared. To my left, the side gate was gone, too. I could now see into the back garden. It was just as untidy as I remembered it. And, more importantly, the wall on which I had been leaning was now returned to its former, un-pebble-dashed, brick state. I could see flakes of red paint peeling off.

Heart beating loudly in my chest, I stood up, wincing when my legs protested – it felt like I'd been sitting in one position for hours.

The first thing I did was look into the side window – and what I saw there made me laugh out loud for joy. The dining room, with its tacky furniture and spotless demeanour, had gone. In its place was my mum's messy, slightly smelly, bedroom – complete with old-fashioned TV and beaten up old wardrobe. My mum's bed was in its usual place, and I could see her figure outlined under the covers, her messy hair just visible on the pillow.

Mum! Until that moment, I don't think I'd ever realised how much she meant to me.

Running now, I hurried round to the front door – yes, it, too, was its dear old self – barely noticing that the front garden and drive were back to normal, and plucked my key out of my pocket. It fitted!

As I opened the door and went inside, I realised I still had the 'stone' in my hand. Carefully, I put it into my back pocket, out of harm's way, making sure not to press any part of it.

Inside was just as I had left it this afternoon – which now seemed so far away it was unreal. There was the worn rug by the front door, there was the old print of a sad-looking dog on the hall wall, there were Lizzie's muddy trainers, and her raincoat on the end of the bannister.

Lizzie! My god, I'd forgotten about Lizzie!

I ran into the living room, where the TV was turned off and empty dishes lay on the arm of the settee. Where was she?

Almost tripping over some Lego left on the floor, I ran towards the stairs and went up them two at a time, before flinging open the door to her room.

She was there, sitting on her bed, reading a comic. I rushed over to her and gave her a big hug, putting my face in her long, blond hair, scared I might cry again.

"What on earth are you doing, Ethan?" Her voice was muffled, and she sounded a little annoyed.

I let her go, suddenly embarrassed.

She looked at me as if I had gone mad. "And where have you been? I had to get mum's tea, and everything!"

She stared at me. "What's wrong? You look like you've seen a ghost."

I smiled at her, not knowing what to say. Maybe I *had* seen a ghost. Or two.

She started to tell me what they'd had for tea – beans on toast, but she'd burnt the toast and had to do it again – and how mum had been extra demanding all evening, requiring her to read a story, and how there was nothing on TV she wanted to watch, and how she'd nearly rung me on my mobile because I'd been out so long... (my sister can go on a bit when she wants to), but by this time I wasn't listening. I glanced up at her pink, princess clock on the wall and was amazed to see it was nearly nine o'clock.

Nine o'clock? Surely I'd only been gone a couple of hours.

Whatever – I was suddenly tired of all this

mystery; all I wanted to do now was go into my familiar bedroom and sleep. But there was one thing I had to ask first.

"Lizzie," I said, shutting her up with a wave of my hand.

"Yes, Ethan?"

"This is going to sound daft, but..." I paused, not sure how to put it.

"What?" she asked, clearly irritated I'd left her on her own with mum all afternoon.

"Did anything *interesting* happen while I was away? Anyone call round? Anything to do with mum or the house or... anything?" I knew what her answer would be before she said it, but I still had to ask.

"No," she said, her little forehead wrinkling up in puzzlement.

I breathed out audibly. I just knew it.

"Except the smoke alarm went off when I burnt the toast, and I had to get a chair to stand on so's I could blow the smoke away with a tea towel, and then mum was shouting at me from her room and I had to tell her what was happening, and..."

Feeling more tired than I had in a long time, I kissed Lizzie goodnight, told her to get to bed and went next door to my room.

Yep, it was still there. The posters on the wall, that hid the damaged wallpaper, were still hanging from their Blu Tack – Doctor Who's TARDIS, a guide to sea birds I'd got out of a newspaper, an old Star Wars poster I'd found in the attic (Jake said it might be worth lots of money some day, but I liked it so much I had to put it up).

My bed, worn-out spring mattress and all, was still in the centre of the room, covered by a slightly faded blue duvet cover; and the chest of drawers was still under the window, bare except for a hairbrush, a football magazine Jake had given me, and a small collection of pebbles and shells from the beach.

Although I was tired, there was something I had to do before I got into bed. I opened the top drawer, the one where I keep my undies and socks, and searched at the back for my special box. Actually an old cigar box – another find from the attic – it held several assorted 'treasures' I didn't want anyone else to see. Some of these I had actually forgotten the meaning of, but I kept them just the same. I took it out now, sat on the bed and opened it on my lap.

Right at the bottom, underneath the drawings, notes and odds and ends – there was my swimming medal from school, a picture of me Lizzie had drawn when she was tiny, a business card from dad's old plumbing days – there was even an acorn in there, I'm not sure why – was the photo of my dad, Lizzie and me.

I took it out and examined it – well, his face, anyway.

Yes. There was no doubt about it. Earlier that day I had seen him, leaving this house.

I put it back in the box, this time on the top, and very carefully added the 'stone' that, I had to conclude, had somehow taken me to another world and – thankfully – back again. Then I closed the lid and put it back in the drawer.

Breathing a sigh of relief, I went to the toilet, then slowly undressed to get into my pyjamas. I took my phone out of my jeans pocket, and was pleased to see it now seemed to be working fine. I thought about calling Jake, but was way too tired to do it now. I climbed into bed. Mystery-solving could wait until tomorrow.

Keeping mum

The next day was Saturday, and I slept late, waking to the sound of the smoke alarm as, I guessed rightly, Lizzie burnt some more toast.

At first I couldn't remember anything about the strange day I'd had – I suppose I put it down to a dream – but suddenly it hit me. It had all been real, hadn't it?

Needing to find out for sure, I got out of bed and rooted about in my undies draw for the treasures box. When I opened it and saw the stone-like device on top, I knew that all the weird stuff had really happened. It just looked alien, somehow – not of this world, at any rate.

I sat there looking at it – I didn't dare touch it again – for some time before Lizzie knocked on my door and startled me. "Ethan, are you awake?" she yelled.

"If I wasn't before, I am now," I replied, smiling to

myself.

After some breakfast, I left Lizzie watching TV in mum's room to keep her company while I went to phone Jake on his mobile. He'd know what to do about my weird experience. He answered straight away. "Yo dude!" he said. Jake was a great friend and very intelligent, but he had no idea how to be cool.

"Hi," I said. "You OK?"

"Sure thing, matey boy. Just going swimming with dad."

"Oh," I said, and I must have sounded a bit upset, because he added: "You could come too, if you like?"

The thing was, any other time I could have gone – would have gone – Jake's family were really kind to me, offering to take me places all the time, but I often said no because it felt too much like I was the poor kid who never went anywhere.

Jake's dad was a lawyer, his mum a vet, his big sister at university and his big brother doing well at secondary school. They were well off, had long holidays and were always going out on day trips, which is why I hardly ever saw my best friend in the summer. Usually I would have leapt at the chance to spend a day with him.

But today was different. I needed his help.

And I needed him here.

So I said: "Thanks, but I can't get out today... I need to tell you something. I need you to see something."

"What? What's the matter? Is it your mum?" he asked, thoughtful as ever.

"No, it's not mum, it's something I can't tell you over the phone." I paused, then: "It could be really important."

Jake was obviously curious. "OK, mystery man. How's about I get dad to drop me off at yours after swimming? Then you can tell me all about it. And you can make me some of that wonderful spaghetti Bolognese of yours for tea."

I laughed. "That would be great," I said, "but I do believe there's only fish fingers and oven chips on the menu tonight."

"That'll do me, matey," he said. "I'll be round about one.

. . . .

Just before lunchtime, I decided I needed to talk to mum. Oh, I wasn't going to tell her what had happened yesterday – oh god, no, she'd cart me off to the doctor's before you could say "what's that strait jacket for?" No, I wanted to ask her about dad.

Mum never talked about him at all. Since he left us, in the middle of the night, she had barely mentioned him. When me and Lizzie asked where he'd gone, she just said: "Away."

We gave up asking after a while.

A year or so back I'd tried to find out why he left, but she shut me up pretty fast, saying she was too tired to speak about it now and that she'd tell me more when I was older.

Well, now I was older.

"Mum?" I knocked gently on her door, as always,

then pushed the door open.

I was pleasantly surprised to see she was actually sitting up, reading a book. This was good – positively energetic for her, recently. The radio was on, too, but she obviously wasn't listening to it, so I turned it off.

"Oi," she said, "I was listening to that."

"No you weren't," I replied, sitting on the chair next to her bed. "You feeling a bit better?"

She looked up from her book, and I could see that she'd been crying. "Not too bad, son," she said. "You going out today?"

I was pleased she was taking an interest. When she was bad, she barely lifted her head up from the pillow and showed no interest in anything. A herd of elephants could have gone past the window and she wouldn't have even blinked.

"No," I said, "but Jake's coming round later and staying for tea." She smiled. This was looking promising. "Good," she said, "I like Jake. Nice polite boy." She paused. "Nice hair," she added.

"Er, yeah..." I wasn't sure how to broach the

subject most on my mind, so talked for a while about the weather, what was on TV that night, how Lizzie must surely be able to make toast without burning the house down – anything and everything I could think of, until she put a thin hand on my arm, and startled me by saying: "What's the matter, Ethan?"

I looked up at her, and was surprised to see she was looking directly at me with her clear, hazel eyes. She looked more alive than she had done in years.

I said nothing. What could I say? That I'd somehow seen dad with a different version of her? It would sound ridiculous. It *was* ridiculous.

So instead I stammered: "I... I wanted to ask about dad." Which was true, anyway.

She sighed and took her hand away. "I thought so," she said, in a quiet voice.

I let her think for a minute, before adding: "I just wanted to know if you knew where he was, what he was doing?"

She grabbed my arm again, this time tightly. "Don't you ever go looking for him, you hear? Ever!"

I was shocked at how loud her voice was, how savage she sounded. Mum was always so gentle and quiet.

"I don't want to do that," I said, upset now. "I just wondered if you knew what he was doing now."

She seemed to calm down, and released my arm. She turned her head away towards the window, and it was a while before I realised she was speaking.

"...knew you'd want to learn more," she was saying. She turned to face me again, and I was startled to see how old she suddenly looked. She was only 36, but life had taken its toll on her face.

"I have no intention of looking for dad, if you don't want us to," I said, meaning it.

She smiled a thin, tired smile. "I know, son," she said. "You're a good boy, Ethan. You look after me and your sister and never complain." Her smile faded, and she looked away again. I think she was trying not to cry. "I've been such a bad mother these last four years," she went on. I tried to say she wasn't, but of course we both knew that would be a lie, so she stopped me with a wave of her hand and went on, her voice stronger: "I have no idea where your dad is, Ethan. I haven't seen him since he left this house four years ago.

"Oh, I heard from him after he left – he rang almost constantly for a month or so, begging to come home, but I stood firm and he soon went quiet. I've not heard a peep since. For all I know he's dead. He never sent us any money, anyhow."

I was shocked to hear her speak like this. The thought raced through my head that *I'd* seen him pretty recently – at least, a version of him – but something else occupied my mind. Begging to come home? I thought he left of his own accord.

I was about to speak, but she went on: "I expect you're old enough to learn the truth, now – you're almost a man, going to big school next month."

I grunted. Tell me about it. I wasn't looking forward to *that* at all.

She was still speaking – on a roll, now she'd decided to tell me what happened.

"Your dad was always a bully, Ethan – I know you

59

don't remember much about it, because you were only young and I shielded you from the worst of it."

Yes, I knew he was a bully, alright. I remembered quite well his shouting, usually at mum but sometimes at me and Lizzie, and his threats.

She was rubbing her head now, like it was hurting her to speak. "He was always demanding this, asking for that, screaming if he didn't get what he wanted. Threatening to hurt me if I disobeyed him." I winced at this. "Well, that night his threats turned into action for the very first time. He hit me, Ethan."

I stared at her, horrified.

"Yes," she said. "It was over something trivial, as usual – the details don't matter anymore – and he was yelling, and I was telling him to be quiet because he'd wake you up, but he wouldn't. And then he hit me, hard, in the face, with the back of his hand. There was blood in my mouth."

I didn't know what to say. What could I?

She went on, sad now: "I stood there for a while, not knowing what to do, and he was saying it was my

60

fault for provoking him – and then it struck me, if you'll pardon the pun," she gave a small chuckle, then stared me straight in the eyes. "If I let him get away with it, that would be just the start. He'd hit me again, maybe not the next day, but certainly sometime soon. And then he'd start on you, too."

I nodded, understanding completely.

"So I showed him the door, told him to get out and never come back or I would call the police. I was really quite surprised he went, but I suppose he could tell I meant it."

She stopped and lay her head back against the headboard, closing her eyes.

"So that's it. That's the story of why your father left, and why I don't want you to try to find him."

I nodded again, unable to speak. It explained so much – why mum never wanted to speak of him, why we'd never had so much as a birthday card since he left; maybe even why she'd fallen into this desperate state. I had a thought. "Mum," I said. "Yes, Ethan?"

"Did you fall ill after dad left?"

She opened her eyes again and seemed to be thinking. "Yes," she said, as if she'd only just thought of it herself. "Not long after."

I nodded again. It seems the stress of what had happened had brought on mum's illness, somehow. She had certainly not been the same since.

I reached over and kissed her cheek. She looked up at me and smiled. "I thought you'd hate me for driving him away," she said. "You're my mum," I said, simply. "He was just a bully."

As I left the room to get her something to eat, she smiled at me from her bed, looking suddenly stronger, and said: "Please don't tell Lizzie. Not yet."

"I won't," I replied, and went to get the lunch ready.

Telling Jake

Jake arrived, as promised, just after one. His hair – longish, blond and curly – was wet from swimming and plastered against his head in an untidy mess. His dad waved from the car and promised to pick him up later.

I got us both a drink of lemonade and took him straight into my bedroom. Mum was having a nap, and Lizzie had gone out to her friend's house down the road for the afternoon.

He sat on the bed and idly pulled at his wet hair with his fingers, trying to untangle it.

"So, what's the big secret?" he asked.

I took a deep breath and sat down next to him. "Actually I have two, but you can only hear one," I smiled, liking the mystery thing. I had no intention of telling him about my dad hitting mum.

He smirked. "OK, then, what do you want to tell

me about?" "I don't know where to start," I said.

"How about the beginning?"

"OK," I laughed, "But promise not to interrupt until I get to the end." "Fine, my lips are sealed," he smiled, doing that zip-up movement near his mouth.

So, slowly, I told him, just like I told you before. About going for a walk to the coastguard house; about finding the 'stone'; the blackout; walking back along the changed footpath; the pig on a lead; the barricaded shop; Mr Hughes and his piggy friend; the different houses; *my* altered house and seeing 'mum' and 'dad'. I didn't leave anything out, not even the bit where I was crying, and by the time I got to the part about finding myself back home, I was really tired and my friend's hair was nearly dry.

Jake, bless him, just sat there, sipping his lemonade, looking at me with eyes that seemed to get wider and wider as the story went on. His mouth fell open when I got to the bit about the shop, and it took a while before he closed it again.

When I'd finished, he sat in silence, thinking, eyes

still wide. I could tell he didn't believe me – why would he believe me? What had supposedly happened to me went against every rule of the universe as we knew it.

I broke the silence. "I'm not mad, you know," I said, a little defensively.

He looked at me, said nothing. I went on: "I know it sounds ridiculous, but it happened. I can't prove it, but it did, and you're the only person I felt I could tell."

He smiled at this, then seemingly had a thought. "This stone-like thing – you've still got it, right?"

Of course I had! But I didn't want to touch it again. "Ye-es," I said.

"But you're frightened of it, right?" he said.

"Oh god, yes," I said. I always told Jake the truth.

"Where is it?"

Reluctantly, I got my treasures box out of my drawer and handed it to Jake. I watched, scared, as he opened it gingerly, as if there was a bomb inside.

The 'stone' was still there, sitting on top of the

box's contents. I think Jake was quite surprised to see it was real. His eyebrows raised, and he stared closely at it. "Oh my..." he whispered, and I knew he could see it, too – that it was not something made in *this* world.

He reached out an index finger to touch it, and I shouted "No!"

He looked at me. "It's OK, Ethan. You touched it – had it in your pocket, and your hand – and nothing happened until you found the button."

"But..." I stammered. Jake continued, as if he'd already given it some thought: "When you first picked it up in the coastguard house, you must have pressed the button by mistake."

I nodded. I understood this, but I was still afraid he'd suddenly be whisked away to another world if he so much as touched a finger to it.

Jake touched a finger to it. I winced. He stroked it with his finger, feeling its weirdly soft surface. Thankfully, nothing happened. "Wow," he said, "It's certainly not a material I've ever seen before. Maybe a type of soft aluminium, or lead, or something."

Suddenly, he picked it up and held it in the palm of his hand, raising it level with his eyes so he could examine it closely. It seemed to glow, the light faintly reflecting on his face. My heart skipped a beat – I really was terrified of it.

"It's heavy, too," he said, "much heavier than it should be." I nodded, suddenly relieved I had someone to share this with. He put it gently down on the bed and seemed lost in thought for a while. I was beginning to think he may actually believe me, but then he said: "I think you had a hallucination, Ethan."

What? A hallucination? "No way," I said, shaking my head as if it would fall off. "What happened to me was absolutely real – as real as you sitting there now."

"Oh, I have no doubt you believe it was real, but really – another world, maybe parallel universes? Sure, some scientists think they exist, but to actually travel between them? Impossible. The laws of physics won't allow us." He seemed to be trying to convince himself, as much as anything. I shook my head again.

"What about the stone?" I asked.

He looked at it out of the corner of his eye, as if he didn't want to acknowledge how alien it was. "I don't know," he faltered. "It certainly looks strange... but time travel?"

"I didn't say I travelled in time," I said, defensive now.

"But you said you seemed to lose a few hours when you went from one world to another. That's time travel, isn't it?" he said.

"I... I suppose," I hesitated. "But it all seemed so real!" I was beginning to wish I'd kept this to myself now. If Jake didn't believe me, who would?

Just then, the doorbell went. I ran downstairs to answer it. I was actually quite relieved that I didn't have to continue this awkward conversation with Jake – how on earth could I convince him that what I'd told him was the truth, other than by pressing that button again?

The man standing at the front door was no-one I recognised. He was quite short, about 40, with a tangle of greying, wavy brown hair falling untidily onto his shoulders. He looked very scruffy, as if he hadn't changed his clothes in weeks, and was wearing a faded pair of jeans, wrecked trainers and a dirty brown jacket on top of an old Iron Maiden t-shirt which looked older than him. His face was that weather-beaten brown you sometimes see in people who work outdoors, and he had stubble on his chin.

But his eyes were what caught my attention. A piercing, clear blue, they looked like they had seen the whole world. And more.

He stared at me intently. "Can I help you?" I asked.

His voice, when he spoke, seemed to match his eyes.

"I think you have something that belongs to me," he said, and held up a stone identical to the one now sitting on my bed next to a bewildered Jake.

The stranger

"I – what did you say?" I stammered, astonished, staring at the stone he held in his hand.

"Well, someone in the house has, anyway," he said. "Can I come in?"

"No," I said, quite sternly, I thought. I had no idea who this man was, and really no wish to find out just now. Life was far too complicated as it was.

He peered at me with those piercing eyes, and I shifted uncomfortably under his gaze.

He changed tack. "Is your mum or dad in?" he asked, putting the hand with the stone in by his side.

I had a standard reply for when strangers asked me this at the door: "Mum's in the bath, and dad will be back soon," I said. It usually put them off. Not this time.

The stranger smiled. "Yeah," he said. "And I'm from the Inland Revenue. You're not a very good liar, sonny. Now, do I have to force my way in to recover my property, or will you be civil and let me in nicely?"

I stood, shocked, as he didn't wait for an answer but pushed past me into the hallway. "Nice house," he said, looking round, "but it could do with a clean."

What a cheek! Judging by his scruffy look he was hardly one to talk about hygiene.

He was heading to mum's bedroom door, so I quickly grabbed him by the arm and stopped him. "Upstairs," I said, deciding playing dumb any longer would be a waste of time, and trying to get him out of the house impossible without making a noise.

He went up two at a time, and I followed. "In there," I said, pointing to my bedroom door. He pushed the door open and went in, as if he owned the place.

"Hello there," I heard him say to Jake, who, I saw, was now holding the stone in the palm of his left hand. Before either of us could speak, the stranger plucked the stone out of Jake's hand with a short "Thank you, I do believe that is mine."

"Oi," said Jake, and, to me, "Who the hell is he?"

I shrugged, just as confused.

The stranger plonked himself down on the floor and sat in a crossed-legs position against the wall, as if meditating. He looked up at us both, staring at him, and said to me: "Sit down, you're making me nervous."

I sat slowly on the bed, next to Jake, who started to say something, but I shushed him. I had never felt so powerless in my own bedroom before.

The man was holding both stones, one in each hand, and as we watched, amazed, he brought them slowly together. As they approached one another, they started to glow brightly, the brightness increasing the closer they got, until they touched – and when they did, there was a bright flash of light, like a camera going off.

Jake and I both gasped, and the stranger laughed, then said: "It's OK, it's just a dispersal of energy. I've been tracking this DART for hours and the energy created needs to go somewhere."

Jake and I stared at him. Dozens of questions raced through my brain: What on earth was he talking about? Who was he? How did he know the stone was here? What the hell was it, anyway?

Before I could say anything, Jake piped up: "Who *are* you? And what are those things?"

The man put his head on one side and seemed to be measuring us up. Instead of answering Jake's questions, he asked one of his own: "Who found it then?"

Scared he might be police or something – despite his appearance – I tried bluffing. "Found what?" I asked.

He smiled and held up the stone in his right hand. "This, dopey," he said. "I know it's mine, because these are the only two in this reality." I jumped at this. Excited, I asked him: "So it *can* take you to other dimensions, then?"

He seemed a bit taken aback. "You didn't use it, did you?" he asked.

I nodded. Jake was alternately staring at me and

73

the stranger, as if watching a really gripping tennis match. I found this very funny, and nearly laughed, but was too intent on finding out what had happened to me the day before.

I didn't want to tell the man any more without knowing who he was, but I was desperate to discover what the device did, so I decided to turn inquisitor instead. "Who *are* you?" I asked.

The man put both stones in the top pocket of his jacket, and carefully buttoned it up. Then he got up, sighed, and headed for the door. "Sorry, sonny, but that's classified." He was going to leave without telling us anything! I just couldn't let that happen.

"Oh no you don't!" I shouted, springing to my feet and barring his way. He was taller than me, obviously much stronger, and I half expected him to throw me to one side and leave anyway, but instead he kind of smirked and backed off.

I pressed home my advantage. "I want to know what that thing is, and where it took me, and... and I'm not letting you leave until you tell me." I said. Jake muttered an amused "hear, hear." I felt like a school teacher keeping a naughty kid in detention.

The man looked amused, and impressed, too, I thought. Slowly he sat down on the floor again, in the same position as before, and gestured for me to sit down, too. I did, half expecting him to make a dash for the door.

But he stayed put this time, sighed deeply and said: "OK, sonny..."

"Ethan," I interrupted. "Ethan Jones. And this here is Jake."

"OK," he resumed. "Mr Jones," and he nodded towards Jake, "and Jake, I suppose I owe you an explanation. At least since I barged my way into your house."

Then he leant his head back against the wall, scratched his nose, sniffed, and said: "But I think if I'm going to tell you all about myself, I'd better have something to drink first."

I stared at him, puzzled.

He went on: "A cup of tea? Coffee? Coke? I'm not

fussy, really – as long as it's not Irn Bru. Evil stuff. Euch!"

"Oh," I said, "OK." And I got up and headed to the door. As I opened it, he shouted after me: "And a bite to eat would be nice. I'm starving."

As quick as I could, I went downstairs, put a few crackers, a bit of cheese and some ham on a plate, poured a large glass of lemonade – I didn't want to waste time making tea, for goodness' sake – and raced back upstairs with them to find the stranger in the same position, picking at his teeth, watched by a silent, obviously dumbfounded, Jake.

I handed the plate and glass to the man, and he fell about them as if he hadn't eaten for weeks, which was, I later found out, close to the truth. Jake and I sat there, looking at him, until he had finished. It didn't take long.

He put the glass down and burped loudly. "That's better," he said, adding: "I could just go a nap now." And he shut his eyes.

"Oh no you don't," I said. "You have to tell us who

you are and why you're here."

He opened his eyes again and smiled. "Sorry," he said. He looked at us both in turn, nodded as if he'd made a decision, and told us his amazing tale.

Sam's story: 1

"My name is Samuel, but most people call me Sam. Except the ones I don't like, who I insist call me Mr Harding." He chuckled at his own joke. This is going to be a long story, I thought.

"I was born 48 years ago in a different reality to this one..." Jake and I both gasped – this was becoming a habit – but he ignored us and went on: "The scientists at I-ART call it reality 367,930,509,022, which is a bit of a mouthful, I admit. I just call it home, myself." He grinned, showing a row of dirty but even teeth. "It's much like this one – a few major changes, nothing too drastic, but the main difference to you is that in my reality we discovered a long time ago that alternative realities exist, and found out how to travel between them via the sub-atomic level."

He paused, and looked at us as if we should be

impressed. Jake obviously was, but I had no idea what he was talking about. Sub-atomic? Samuel sighed and went on: "OK, I can see you haven't a clue what I'm talking about, so let's put it simply."

"Yes please," I said, "as simply as possible would be nice."

He smiled again. "OK," he repeated. "Let's begin with a physics lesson. Everything in the universe is made up of particles – atoms, most of us call them – and every atom is made up of a number of smaller particles: the bigger ones, protons, neutrons and electrons, are in turn made up of a whole string of other particles, which all interact on each other in many and varied ways, some of which we still don't know. This small level of reality is called sub-atomic, because it's smaller than atomic, get it?"

I nodded for him to go on. "About 50 years ago, in my reality, we discovered that sub-atomic particles can exist in millions of places at the same time. After a while, that discovery led to us realise that whenever a *sizeable* number of particles makes a drastic move or change – we still don't understand it properly, I'm sorry to say – then an alternative reality is created. And when I say a sizeable number of particles, I mean something as big as a human, say.

"So alternative realities are created all the time, as far as we understand it – every time a human being or something larger than a human does something out of the ordinary.

"Every time an elephant, say, kills a human out of anger; when a volcano erupts; when a war is lost or won; when a large meteorite crashes to earth; every time someone decides to emigrate to Australia instead of stay at home in Stoke. When a centuries-old tree comes crashing down unexpectedly during a storm. We're not sure exactly what triggers it, but when it does, it makes a whole new world."

"So there must be millions of them, right?" piped up Jake. He sounded excited.

"Countless billions," replied Samuel. "We don't know how many, and we're not even sure of the rules governing them, yet. But they exist, alright. All sitting side by side, just a sub-atomic level away. Never touching."

"But you can travel between them? In your reality?" asked Jake.

Samuel nodded. "Easy as pie," he said. "How?" asked Jake.

Samuel paused, then pointed to his buttoned-up top pocket, where the stone-like devices were safely ensconced. "With these," he said slowly, as if he was talking to a really dumb person.

"I gathered that," said Jake, "But how?"

Samuel pulled a face. "*I* don't know!" he said, "I'm not a scientist."

"Well, what are you then?" I asked, suddenly afraid he may be some sort of intergalactic police or something.

"I'm an agent," said the stranger. "An agent for I-ART." "Who?" I asked.

Samuel sighed again. I think he was bored by all this explaining – but he wasn't doing it very well, I thought.

"I-ART is the Institute for Alternative Reality Technology, based in London. They're the ones who've got all the clever-dick scientists with the big ideas. They developed the DARTs..." he held up his hand to silence Jake's question, and went on: "DART stands for Device for Alternative Reality Transportation. Yeah, I know it's a crap name, but they liked the idea of saying we can DART from one reality to the other, see?"

Jake and I both nodded. Encouraged, he continued: "The DARTs can be programmed to take us to any of millions of alternative realities, at the touch of a button. We agents – there were 50 of us when we started all this 18 years ago – are sent into different realities to do research; find out what similarities and differences exist in which reality; what lessons can be learnt; discover what makes other realities a success or otherwise – you know, all good stuff."

"So you've travelled to lots of different realities?" asked Jake, rather unnecessarily, I thought.

Samuel looked at him as if he was an idiot.

"Dozens," he said.

"And?" Jake went on. "What were they like?"

Samuel yawned. "Mostly dull," he said.

I was beginning to think this conversation was like getting blood out of a stone. Thankfully, Samuel elaborated a bit. "Most of them are nothing special – in some of them it's hard to find any differences at all, unless you want to spend years there, and we weren't allowed to do that – six months at the longest in each place was all we got.

"But some *are* worth writing home about. Like the ones where the wheel was a new invention; oh, and the ones where the Nazis won the Second World War – whoo, they're pretty scary. Though the trains do run on time..." he went quiet again, lost in thought, so I asked him: "What's the most interesting one you've ever been to?"

He thought for a bit, then replied: "Probably the one where man didn't exist."

Jake jumped – actually, physically jumped. "What?" he asked.

Samuel seemed to like the attention this had got him. "Oh yeah," he said. "That was a good one. Well, not good, exactly. The dinosaurs were a bit annoying; some of them wouldn't leave me alone; and it was hard to find enough food – no McDonald's, you see." He grinned at his own wit.

"Dinosaurs?" Jake and I asked together.

Samuel went on grinning. "Indeed," he said. "There are millions of realities in which the dinosaurs were never wiped out – perhaps the climate change never happened, or the meteorite never struck – we're still not sure what was the cause of it. Anyway, in those realities homo sapiens never came about – the dinosaurs just evolved, instead. Not very far, I'm afraid to say..." he rubbed his chin thoughtfully, "They never became very intelligent. Still not got round to making fire."

He stopped and looked around him, as if he was getting bored. To stop him going, I asked him another question: "How did you find out I had your – what did you call it? DART?"

"Yeah, DART," he replied. "That's easy. Us agents always keep a spare one on us, and they can home in on each other – in case we lose one, it sends out a signal to the missing one. Like a homing device, if you like. So as soon as I noticed it had gone, I set about following its signal, which led me here."

A question seemed to occur to him, and he looked at me. "Where did you find it?" he asked.

"In the old coastguard house, down on the beach," I said.

He nodded. "Yeah, I've been staying there for a couple of days, now. It's not very pleasant, but at least it's dry."

Jake asked the next one: "How long have you been in our reality?" Samuel looked sheepish. "A while," he said.

"How long?" I asked. Samuel changed position on the floor, putting his legs out in front of him. He sighed. "About nine months," he said.

I must have looked puzzled – didn't he say the agents only stayed in each place for six months? – for he followed it with: "Yeah, I know. Too long."

"What happened?" I asked.

Samuel sighed again. "Nine months ago the agent branch of I-ART was shut down due to lack of government funding. We've had the same economic crisis as your reality, see. The big wigs decided alternative realities were costing too much and not producing the goods – 18 years and still no cures for cancer or AIDS, no hugely useful technology, no insights into eradicating poverty. All the agents were supposed to hand over their DARTs and go looking for another job."

I interrupted him: "But you didn't want to."

He grinned again. "Who could give all this up for a life on benefits? This had been my life for 18 years. I had no other. The day we were supposed to finish up, I DARTed here. I've been living rough ever since."

It was Jake's turn for a question. "Won't they come and find you? I mean, can't they trace your... DART?"

Samuel laughed. "Oh they wouldn't bother doing that. The DARTs only take the bundle of particles connected to them when the button is pressed – a person, for instance – and they're not easily traceable across realities. It can be done, but takes a lot of time and effort, so I-ART never knew where we had gone on a mission until we returned. It was just a random number on the DART. That's partly why they lost so many."

I said: "Sorry? Lost so many what?"

"Agents," Samuel replied. "In the first five years of operating alone 23 of them disappeared. Some of them probably got killed – DARTed straight into the arms of a hungry dinosaur or an armed Nazi or something – but many probably just felt the life they saw in the other reality was better than their own. It was an occupational hazard. Turnover of agents was pretty fast – some couldn't take it. That's why I-ART only used agents with no family and few friends – so no-one would kick up a fuss if they never came back."

"So you have no family then? No-one to go back to?" I asked.

The former agent shook his head. "I can't go back

now, anyway."

"Why?" I asked.

Samuel looked straight at me from under his long fringe. His bright blue eyes, which had clearly seen far more than I ever would, seemed to look right into me.

"Because they'd probably kill me."

Sam's story: 2

"Kill you?" Jake asked, astonished. Surely Samuel's reality wasn't that far removed from ours – he'd said so himself.

Samuel nodded seriously. "Penalty for deserting my duty. Like treason, if you like – do you have that term here?" Jake nodded: "Yeah, but we don't kill anyone for it anymore," he said.

Samuel shrugged. He went on: "As soon as I DARTed back home they'd trace me – no matter how far away I was from London, they'd find me within a few hours. Five, tops. And it would be death by firing squad, no questions asked. Well, I might get a trial first."

"But that's barbaric!" I shouted. Samuel shrugged again. "That's my reality," he said. "Compared to some of the ones I've seen, it's positively humane."

The three of us fell silent, and Samuel looked at his

watch. "Anyway," he said, "Can't sit around here all day chin-wagging... well, actually, I could, as I have nothing better to do." He grinned again, and I was suddenly struck by how likeable this man was. He'd been in my house less than an hour and I didn't want him to go.

Jake was beginning to look agitated. I was sure he, too, didn't want Samuel to leave – how much he could tell us about other worlds! To a scientific brain like Jake this was like having Einstein in the same room.

My friend confirmed this by saying: "How about staying for tea? Ethan here makes a great lasagne."

Samuel looked tempted – when I came to think of it, he looked like he hadn't eaten for days – but he said: "Lasagne sounds great, lads, but won't your mum and dad be back soon? How would you explain an old tramp like me sitting with my feet under the table?"

I laughed. "You don't have to worry about that," I said. "My dad left home years ago and mum's almost bed-bound.

"I'm the chef round here. Jake is just visiting."

Samuel grinned again. He did that a lot. "Lasagne it is, then!" he said.

It was my turn to look sheepish. "Er, actually, it's fish fingers and chips. And beans, if we have any," I said.

The rest of that afternoon passed like a blur. Samuel sat on the floor, telling us tales of his adventures in other worlds – some we didn't believe, but I think, on reflection, they were all true – and Jake and I sat next to each other on the bed, getting pins and needles in our legs through not moving, but not caring in the least.

This stranger further explained about his life, and his reality. Before becoming an agent, he had been in the army for a while, and then was taken on as a personal bodyguard for some big name in business. He got married in his twenties, but had no children, and then his wife had died from cancer at the age of just 28. It was this that made him volunteer for the I-ART project. "I reckoned if I could find a cure for cancer, which was one of the biggest I-ART goals, I could save millions of people from going through what I did," he said, simply.

I asked him what the biggest discovery was he had made. Straight away, he said: "A new way of making oil go further. I was really lucky with that one. Made me a lot of money, and saved my reality from ruining the planet."

Jake said, rather cruelly, I thought: "You don't look like you've got a lot of money."

Samuel laughed. "Not here, I haven't. It's no use to me now. I don't exist here, remember?"

Jake asked: "Aren't you afraid you'll run into another you, here?"

Samuel shook his head. "Can't," he said. "You can only DART into a reality your own particles don't already exist in. If you programme it for one in which you *do* exist, it just bleeps an error message at you and you go nowhere. So no, I've never met myself – and I never can, more's the pity. Now that would make for a great conversation."

I started at this. "So the reality I visited didn't have me in it at all?" I asked.

Samuel looked at me. "No. Your own special, unique combination of particles can never be replicated in any one reality. It physically cannot happen. So the only ones we can visit are ones without us – where, for whatever reason, we were never born, or where we've already died."

I was a little shocked at this. It seems I really had seen my mum and dad in another reality – one in which they never had me, or, worse, one in which I had died young. This made me quite sad, for some reason.

Samuel broke the silence: "So tell me what happened when you found my DART – where did you go?" he asked.

So I told him, quickly and without the bits about being scared and upset – I didn't want to look like a big baby or anything. He nodded when I mentioned the blackout, smiled when I told him about the pigs, and frowned when I told him about coming home and finding dad here.

After I had finished, he said: "That was *my* reality you were in, kid. The DART takes an agent back home once you've been somewhere – it's like a failsafe, so you always get back safely – like a return ticket, if you like. That's why I'm stuck here. I can't use the DARTs to go to another reality, because if I press them, they'll just take me home. *You* could go somewhere else if you programmed the DART first, because the failsafe just applies to the owner – ie, me. But you didn't programme it, so it took you to my reality."

I understood. Presumably I-ART would want all its agents to return safely and not go zooming around endlessly between realities. I was about to ask him why he chose this reality to run away to, when Jake beat me to it. Samuel blushed. It made his tan deeper. "I...er... I didn't, really," he said. We looked at him expectantly, and he went on reluctantly: "I was supposed to go to a reality I'd been to before, where I'd had a great time. Britain in that one is warmer, friendlier, and there's no need for anyone to work because robots do everything. Most things are free, and everyone's at peace. Life is one great big party. I spent all of my allotted six months there, I can tell you." He stopped. "What happened?" I asked.

Samuel grinned again, but this time there was a sadness in his eyes, too. "I messed up," he said. "In the rush to escape I must have keyed the reality identity number in wrong – I think I just got one digit out – and I ended up here. And now I'm here forever."

I grimaced, but Jake said: "Well, it could have been worse." We both looked at him. He went on: "It could have been the dinosaurs." We all laughed, then I thought of something that had been bothering me from the start.

"So what's this with the pigs, then?" I asked. "In your world, I mean?"

Samuel smiled. "They're our pets," he said. "Like you have dogs, we have pigs. Both animals are domesticated, and early on in their history our reality must have decided pigs made good pets and workmates, while you chose the dogs, instead."

"So do you have dogs too, in your world?" Jake asked.

Samuel pulled an amused face. "Er, yeah," he said.

"And?" "Well, the roles are reversed, aren't they? We breed them in farms like you do with pigs." I realised what he meant. "You eat them?" I asked, astonished.

Samuel had the grace to look uncomfortable. "Yeah," he said, adding, as if it made it any better, "They're very tasty."

Jake made a 'vomiting' noise in his throat, but I was OK with the idea. After all, pigs are intelligent animals, too – and even in our reality, some cultures find eating dogs normal.

A joke occurred to me, and I couldn't resist saying it out loud: "So I suppose hot dogs are a totally different thing in your reality?"

Jake groaned, but Samuel was good enough to laugh.

I had thought of another question: "Why did I appear to lose a few hours when I travelled from one

96

reality to the other?" Samuel rolled his eyes. "You kids," he said, "Full of questions." But I think secretly he was pleased to have someone to share this with.

"Well, why?" asked Jake. "Do you travel through time, as well?" The idea of time travel, of course, was just as exciting as that of alternative realities – even more so, maybe. Samuel got up from the floor to stretch his legs. I must admit mine were getting tired, too.

"No, time travel is, as far as we know, impossible," he said. "Time is constant throughout the realities – when we DART to a land with dinosaurs, it's not one millions of years ago but one that exists now. The time lapse is because it takes a while for your particles to travel to another reality – the longer it takes, the further away from *your* reality it is. So, say, it takes a couple of hours to get to a similar reality, but can take 24 hours to get to one which diverged millions of years ago – like the dinosaur ones."

"And what happens to your body in your own reality?" asked Jake, obviously on a roll now. "Does it stay there, too?"

"No, it physically travels through what we call inter-reality space – or IRS for short – the particles are transported, literally disappear from one reality and appear in another. Along with whatever is attached to it – in other words, you take your clothes, belongings you have on you – oh, and anyone else you happen to be holding onto at the time!"

"Weird," said Jake. "It's kind of freaky the first few times you watch, yeah," said Samuel.

At this point I heard mum shouting from downstairs, and looking at the clock I realised it was probably time I got the tea ready, so I reluctantly left Samuel and Jake to discuss science further while I went downstairs, my head reeling with all the information I had taken in.

Making friends

We ate our tea in the kitchen – it's big enough to have a table and four chairs on one side – and mum ate in her bedroom, as usual, so there was no worry about her seeing Samuel. Lizzie wasn't due back for a couple of hours yet.

As I expected, our visitor ate like he hadn't seen a proper meal in days, which I suspect was true. After all, he'd been living rough for months, with no money, and no friends or family to turn to for help.

When he'd had a second helping – I made extra – he sat holding his stomach, groaning softly, sipping at his second cup of tea and looking content. He had by now removed his jacket, and I could see his t-shirt was full of holes.

I wanted to ask him so many questions about the places he'd been to, but as I supposed he would soon be leaving, I concentrated on the here and now instead.

"Samuel?" I asked. He looked at me, and mumbled: "Sam – anyone who feeds me is a friend."

I smiled. "Sam?" I started again.

"Yes, Ethan?" he replied, before belching loudly. "Oops, pardon," he said.

"What are you going to do now? I mean, how will you live? Where will you go?"

He seemed to think this over before replying: "Well, I've had a lot of time to think about that one, and I'm rather at a loss, to be frank."

"What do you mean?" asked Jake, pouring himself another glass of lemonade.

Sam sighed and put down his mug of tea. "I mean, Jakey old boy, that I've been here nine months already and I'm still living in a hovel with no money, no clothes and no way out of here," he said.

"You mean because you don't exist you can't get a job or a house or anything?" asked Jake. Sam nodded, and went on: "You see, when we were sent on a mission for I-ART we had resources like money and identity at our disposal – we took lots of things with us, just in case, but if we needed anything particularly, we could just DART back home and get it made specially. For instance, like I think I told you before, I once transported into a version of Britain in which the Germans had won the Second World War and had taken over the whole of Europe. In that case, I needed to go back home pronto for a crash course in the language and German identity papers."

Jake interrupted him: "The Germans won the war? What happened to Hitler?"

Sam yawned. "Oh he died an old man, surrounded by flunkies and stolen art – at least, in that reality – and his son came to power. Ruled over Europe with an iron fist. Not a nice place to be, that one... anyway, in that case, I could get help when I needed it. Now, although I brought some stuff with me, none of it is any use, because I came to the wrong place, and I can hardly go back home, can I? So I have to steal or beg to survive. I've managed to get a few odd jobs that pay in cash, but they never last long."

"That must be terrible," said Jake, flicking his long hair out of his eyes and helping himself to a biscuit.

Sam joined him. "Yup," he said, through a mouthful of crumbs, "It's not much fun."

Suddenly I made a decision. "I could help you," I said, excited. Sam looked at me and raised his eyebrows. "I could bring you food and stuff, you know, get you some clothes."

The man smiled. "That's very kind," he said, "but I can't rely on a young lad for the rest of my life. I have to find a way out of this mess."

I was a little disappointed. "Well," I said, "I could at least help you for a little while – until you decide what you're going to do, anyway."

Sam nodded, and agreed this would be nice. "But I have to give you something in return," he said, "because I never take without giving."

Straight away Jake surprised me by saying: "You could let us use your DART!"

Sam shook his head. "No way," he said, "It's far too dangerous. You could end up anywhere."

Jake pressed him: "But Ethan's already DARTed once, and you could show us how to use it properly – you said yourself we can always come home if we need to."

Sam faltered. Obviously his naturally great desire to have clothes on his back and food in his stomach were already persuading him this might be a good idea. I wasn't sure I wanted to go anywhere other than the corner shop ever again, but the idea naturally excited me. What young boy wouldn't want an adventure in a different reality if they had the chance?

So I said: "Jake's right. How about if you let us DART once, back to your reality again, or one you know is safe, and in return I promise to find you some old clothes and feed you until you need to move on?"

I didn't really expect him to say yes, but he really must have been desperate. I suppose living rough with no hope of change does that to even the most resourceful of men, for he said: "OK boys. I'll let you DART once, just to my reality, and under strict conditions, so I can come and rescue you if you get into trouble."

Jake punched the air. "Yes!" he shouted.

And that's where our adventure *really* began. But before we could get too excited, there was an unexpected noise at the kitchen door, and in walked mum.

She was dressed in her tatty brown dressing gown, old slippers on her feet, hair dishevelled and unwashed. She looked worse than Samuel.

"M-mum!" I stuttered, getting up from my chair. She looked round at us all, looking bewildered.

"I've been calling you for ages," she said to me, while her eyes stayed on the stranger with his legs under her table. "I wanted another cup of tea."

I feel dreadful saying it now, but I was ashamed of her – of how she looked, of her reliance on me, of her reluctance or inability to be a proper mum – and I was also scared of her finding out about Sam.

Before I could say anything, Samuel stood up, offered mum his hand to shake and said: "Mrs Jones, I presume. I'm Sam Harding. Pleased to meet you."

Mum looked startled but shook his hand nonetheless, pulling her dressing gown more round herself with her free hand. She seemed dumbstruck, but I was sure she was also blushing.

Sam went on: "I'm so sorry to arrive unannounced, but your son was kind enough to invite me to have a little bite to eat when I brought our Jake round earlier, and we've been having such a good old chat I forgot the time. We really must be going soon, mustn't we, Jake, and leave these good people to themselves?"

He looked expectantly at Jake, who was staring at him as if he'd suddenly grown another head. "Er, yeah," said Jake, clearly not knowing what else to say.

Mum seemed to have regained some of her composure, for she said: "You brought Jake round?"

"Yes," said Sam, "I'm his cousin – once removed – up from London for the week. Our side of the family don't get to see Jakey much, so it's been nice to catch up with the gossip. Anyway, we won't intrude any longer. Come along, Jake, grab your coat and let's get you home again."

I smiled to myself. Samuel really was good at this sort of thing. I suppose he was used to talking his way out of awkward situations.

Mum seemed to accept his story, and was actually trying to get Samuel and Jake to stay longer – god forbid she had a proper conversation with them both; Jake would be bound to give everything away – but soon they were heading out of the front door together. Before they left, I managed to whisper "ring me later" to Jake and "I'll come and see you tomorrow" to Sam, all the while grinning like an idiot at how funny this was all becoming.

When they had left – Jake, presumably, would ring his dad and ask to be picked up – I made mum a cup of tea and took it into her bedroom, where she'd returned. I thought the excitement of finding a stranger in the house had been too much for her, but she was sitting in her chair and looked more animated than I'd seen her for ages.

"You OK, mum?" I asked.

She smiled at me. "You didn't tell me Jake had

106

such a handsome cousin," she said.

I started. "Er..." was all I could say, but she went on: "What a nice man. I wonder if he'd like to come round to tea again before he leaves?"

I smiled back. "I'm certain he would," I said. And boy, did I mean it.

A helping hand

Jake phoned me just after he got home. He'd rung his dad on his mobile and asked him to pick him up from the village shop, giving an excuse that he wanted to buy some sweets on the way home. His dad was none the wiser.

Jake wanted to know whether mum was suspicious.

"Of course not," I said, "Samuel was very convincing."

Jake was so excited by our encounter with a man from another world that he chattered on for ages, going over everything Sam had said, speculating about what this meant for science and our reality – that bit went over my head, I have to admit – and wondering what we'd find when we DARTed to Sam's reality, if he really would let us.

He went on so long his dad told him to get off his

phone, and he had to sign off. I must say I was quite glad. I was tired, emotionally exhausted after the last couple of days' excitement, and just wanted to watch TV for a bit and forget about adventures for a while.

Amazingly, mum joined me and Lizzie – who had returned from her friend's with a full stomach and her hair in plaits – in the living room to watch telly for a couple of hours before bed. I couldn't remember the last time she had felt well enough to do that, and Lizzie and I kept looking at each other and smiling as mum shouted at the TV during some rubbish reality show.

I slept well that night.

....

The next day was sunny but windy. I got mum and Lizzie some breakfast then, pretending I was cleaning the room, went upstairs to what used to be mum and dad's bedroom before he left.

Except for hoovering and dusting every now and then, I hadn't spent time in that room for years, but I knew what I was after. I went to the old wardrobe and looked inside. Yep, they were still there – dad's old clothes. I knew he'd left some, if not all, of them behind when he vanished from our lives, and I thought most of them would fit Sam very well.

I grabbed an old sports bag from the top of the wardrobe, gave it a quick dusting down then filled it with as many clothes as I could cram in – t-shirts, a couple of pairs of jeans, two old sweatshirts, a black shirt, socks – there was even a pair of trainers, and though I didn't know Sam's size I thought I may as well take them, too. I was going to leave the underpants, as I thought no-one would want those, no matter how desperate they were, but then I came across a packet of three new boxer shorts, unopened, and threw them in, too.

The bag was heavy, but I managed to lug it onto the top of the wardrobe again, where it didn't look too different from before. I'd get it later, but first I had to get together some food to take. That shouldn't be too hard, as I did all the shopping and cooking and mum never knew what we had in the cupboards – all I had to do was wait until the coast was clear.

My chance came after lunch, when mum, who'd actually got dressed and come into the kitchen for a bit, went for a lie down and Lizzie went to play dolls upstairs in her room.

Quickly, I grabbed a rucksack from under the stairs and filled it with canned goods – beans, hot dogs, spaghetti hoops, soup – and some fresh stuff like bread rolls and a packet of ham. I even threw in a handful of tea bags and a packet of biscuits. Then I sneaked out of the back door and put the rucksack behind the bins, where I could collect it later.

Getting the bag of clothes downstairs proved more trouble, as I had to wait for Lizzie to go into the toilet before I could chance it, but soon I was heading out of the door with it on my back, after calling to Lizzie that I was going for a walk and would be back before tea.

The trek to the old coastguard house had never been so painful. The rucksack on my back was very heavy, from all the cans, and the bag of clothes on one shoulder kept digging in so much I had to keep stopping for a rest. Nevertheless, I got there in the end, thankfully without being seen by anyone I knew. I had never been so pleased to reach a destination in all my life.

I hurried through the overgrown garden and around the back, calling softly as I reached the back door, which was open: "Sam?" There was no answer, so I added: "It's me, Ethan. I've brought you something."

Suddenly he appeared in the doorway, beaming. I jumped, then smiled back.

"Come on in," he said, beckoning me inside, "My door is always open – mainly because it won't shut anymore, but that's beside the point, don't you think?"

I laughed and stepped into the grimy kitchen, lugging my precious cargo behind me. "A little help wouldn't go amiss," I said, "I've had to carry this all the way from home."

Sam started and grabbed the bag from my shoulder. "Ruddy hell, Ethan old boy," he said, "have you got the kitchen sink in here, or what?"

We went through to the living room, with its dirty bare floorboards and old fireplace, and Sam and I both put down our loads. I told him what I'd brought, and he spent a few minutes going delightedly through the contents of both bags, grinning at the boxers – "Gosh, it'll be nice to get a fresh pair of these on," he said – and holding the cans of food up like they were trophies. I think he was a bit dumbstruck, and I could've sworn there was a tear or two in his eye.

Embarrassed, I rambled on a bit about what else I could bring him when I got the chance – matches, cutlery, an old pan or two, cleaning materials, some soft drinks from the shop – and then stopped as I realised he was looking at me in a strange way. "What?" I asked, and was surprised when he suddenly grabbed me in a bear hug. I can't say I hugged him back – I'm not used to affection – and I was pleased when he quickly let me go again.

When he did, he said: "That's the nicest thing anyone's done for me in a long while."

I looked at him, and he seemed to be welling up again, so I said: "It's nothing, really. No-one wants the clothes – mum just never got round to throwing them out – and the food isn't much, but it may last you a week or so."

Sam was looking round the room, as if he was trying not to cry, and rubbed his nose with the back of his hand. "I wish I could ask you to sit down, but I don't even have a chair," he said, adding: "In fact, I have nothing at all."

I found this hard to argue with – after all, he was right, but I tried: "Well," I said, "as of yesterday, you have two new friends. Isn't that better than nothing?"

Samuel grinned – it was nice to see him smiling again – and started taking the stuff I'd brought through to what was clearly his bedroom – the room in which I'd found the DART and been transported to another world. It was quite strange to be back, knowing what

I now did. I could see that Sam had tidied up – he'd put the rubbish outside, and had cleaned his pans. There was a small but neat pile of plates and bowls next to the cooking stove, and a bottle of Coke next to a collection of plastic cups. The sleeping bag was where it had been before, and I noticed a torch sitting on top of a rucksack in the corner of the room.

I was still telling Sam what I could get him – like most houses, ours had plenty of unused items gathering dust which he may as well put to good use – when he interrupted me. "I don't want to scrounge off you," he said.

I was a little surprised. "You're not scrounging," I replied. "I know you'd look after yourself if you could, but you can't. I want to help you."

Sam sat down on his sleeping bag, and gestured for me to do the same. There was nowhere else to sit. He seemed to think a moment, then said: "I've never been in this position before. In the past, if I got into difficulties, I could just DART home. Sure, I've had to live on next to nothing before, and been in trouble many, many times, but this is something different.

"I'm lost in a world I don't fully understand, with no hope of going home, and no way of bettering my situation."

I suddenly thought of something. "Couldn't you just DART back home, set it to go to somewhere else, then zap off again before the baddies could trace you?" I was surprised at my sudden inspiration.

But Sam was shaking his head. "Our DARTs were to be put out of action, remember? In my reality reprogramming it wouldn't work – in fact, I was surprised it let you come back here. I thought once I returned home it would be unusable. I suppose the return function still works."

"Well, couldn't you go to the police, or government, or someone," I said, "and tell them what you told us? They'd probably make you rich, with all the knowledge you could pass on."

Samuel smiled grimly. "I could," he said, "but I have no desire to become a caged curiosity." I looked quizzically at him. He explained: "They'd lock me up,

116

first of all, as a lunatic. Then, when they discovered what I said was true, they'd treat me as some sort of laboratory rat. Might even do experiments on me, to see how I was different to them."

I shook my head, but he nodded: "Oh yes, don't underestimate the fear people have for anything that's not the same as them," he said. "A person from another world? I'd be treated like an alien. A bug-eyed one with green antennae."

I laughed, but knew he was right.

We passed an hour or so chatting, him telling me funny stories about places he'd visited, me mostly listening, fascinated. As we were talking my mobile rang. It was Jake.

"Yo dude," he said. "How's it going with our man from another world?"

I told him I was with said man at the moment, and he sounded gutted. "I'm missing out on all the fun," he said, and went on to explain he'd been on a family day out to the museum all day. "And dad said I can't come round to yours again until Wednesday," he added – today was Sunday – "because we've got things planned until then."

I sympathised, and he made me promise I wouldn't do anything about DARTing until he was there – as if! There was no way I was going to do that on my own again – and he rang off.

"Sorry about that," I said to Sam. He was pouring himself a cup of Coke, and offered me one. I took it thankfully. It was warm, but welcome nonetheless.

"No problem," he said. I told him what Jake had said, and he frowned. "You know," he said slowly, sitting down again, "I'm not sure about this letting you DART thing."

I looked at him and raised my eyebrows. He shifted his gaze and went on: "You're just boys, you don't know what to do if you're in trouble, and I'd feel terrible if something happened to you."

I wasn't surprised by this change of heart, but – more for Jake's sake than my own – I started to argue: "We're not babies," I said, "We'd only go for a look, not to get into trouble. And you said yourself all we have to do is push the button and we can DART back home."

Sam was shaking his head. I knew he'd take a lot of convincing, but I had to try. "Just one trip," I said, adding, somewhat desperately, "You promised."

He looked at me, lips tight together. I know he was torn between wanting to keep us safe and not wanting to take things off me without paying me back somehow – and how could he pay me back otherwise? Suddenly he closed his eyes, sighed, and said: "OK. Just once – and I tell you where and when."

I punched the air, though part of me wished I'd lost the argument.

Jake's mistake

It was Wednesday, and Jake was coming round for the day. I had managed a few trips to see Samuel that week, and had taken him all manner of things to make his life a bit more comfortable – liquid soap, deodorant, blankets and a pillow, shaving gear, cooking utensils and matches, more food and drink, an old radio we never used anymore, even a few books to read – so he had cleaned himself up and looked less like a tramp than he had before.

I was pleased about this, as mum had asked me to invite "Jake and his charming cousin" over for lunch that day, and I didn't want her becoming suspicious. I knew Jake wanted to DART today – he could barely contain his excitement on the phone when I said Samuel was coming for lunch as well as him.

"Where do you think he's going to let us go?" he asked me, for the umpteenth time. I sighed. "Look," I said, "He's already told us we can only go to his reality, as it's safer all round. He's not going to let us DART to a dinosaur-filled valley or a Nazi country, is he?"

Jake was obviously disappointed at this, though I was scared stiff at the prospect of going anywhere.

Lunch was pleasant enough, though a bit strange. We ate in the kitchen, as usual – mum's bedroom being the old dining room. Samuel fussed over Lizzie and mum, charming them with made-up stories about his life, Jake stayed mostly silent – on strict instructions, in case he let something slip – and mum, who'd been up and dressed for the previous two days, was embarrassingly girly and giggly. I couldn't be sure, but I thought she may even have put some make-up on. Weird.

I busied myself getting food and drink and making sure everyone had enough, but afterwards Sam rose from the table and offered to wash up. Mum, amazingly, said she'd help, and they both started clearing away while Jake and I went into the lounge with our drinks and a plate of chocolate biscuits.

Lizzie excused herself and went upstairs to play, and Jake let out a huge gasp of relief.

"I think I'm going to burst," he said.

I looked at him. "The lunch wasn't that bad, was it?" I asked.

He pulled a face. "No, idiot," he said, "I mean not being able to say anything."

"Oh." I helped myself to another biscuit and offered the plate to Jake. He shook his head. "I'm too excited," he said. I shrugged, saying "all the more for me, then," and stuffed one in my mouth.

It was half an hour before mum and Sam joined us in the living room. Mum looked flushed but tired, and as Sam sat by me on the settee she stood by the door. "I'm going to go for a little lie down," she said. "You boys will entertain Sam, won't you?"

I smiled at her. "Of course we will, mum," I said, though it was more probable Sam would entertain *us*. As she shut the door Sam turned to me. "Your mum's a lovely woman, Ethan," he said, helping himself to a biscuit off the plate.

I didn't really know what to say to this, so I sort of grunted. He carried on: "She's got a great sense of humour." As he said this, I noticed he looked serious, not amused, and I was puzzled. He paused, took a bite of his biscuit, and went on: "It was ME you said she had, wasn't it?"

I nodded, unsure where this conversation was heading. Just then Jake interrupted. "Sam," he said, "I can't bear it any longer. When can we DART? And where? And for how long? And will you have to come with us, or what? And..."

Sam held up his hand. "Woah there tiger," he said, "slow down." Jake shut up. Sam looked at me, then back at my friend, who was sitting on the edge of his chair with excitement. "I know I promised," he started slowly, but Jake interrupted him again: "You can't go back on your word. It's not fair! This is the most interesting and important thing that's ever happened to me – maybe the most important thing ever in the history of this reality – and you're going to deny me the chance to experience it for myself?" He looked furious.

Sam held his hand up again, and smiled. "I didn't say I wouldn't let you," he said. "It's just we need to do it in a measured way, in a safe place, at a safe time." Jake seemed to calm down, and Sam went on: "I need to pick the time and place, that's all. And no, I won't be going with you – remember, as soon as I DART back home, the guys from I-ART will be on my tail. And we don't want that, do we?" He grinned. "Soon, Jakey boy, soon."

Just then Lizzie came in, and we had to change the subject. After a while, she said she wanted to watch the TV, so we let her put it on and decided to go upstairs to my bedroom instead, so we could talk freely. This having to be secret lark was bad for my nerves.

Jake and I sat on my bed while Samuel dropped cross-legged to the floor. He seemed to be comfy like that. For a while we chatted about differences in our worlds, trying to discover more, laughing at some and frowning at others. It was about three o'clock when Jake suddenly asked if he could see the DART again, and maybe hold it.

Sam reached into his jacket pocket and pulled one out. He handed it to me first, as I was closer, and I took it gingerly, turning it over in my hand gently as if it would break.

I hadn't seen it for a while, and I was stunned anew at how alien it looked. Heavy yet smooth, it shone gently onto my palm.

Jake was asking all sorts of technical questions about how it worked, most of which Sam couldn't answer – "Hey, you can use a computer but I bet you don't know how it actually works, do you?" was his reply – then when I passed it to him he went quiet.

I watched as he turned it over and over in his hand, gazing at its delicate hologram-like pattern and tracing it with his finger.

After a couple of minutes he spoke up: "So if I pressed this button, which I can barely see, it will take me back to your reality, in this particular space – ie, the equivalent of Ethan's bedroom in his mum's house?"

Sam nodded. "Yup," he said.

Jake went on: "And to me it would appear to take a moment or two, but in reality would take me a few hours, by Ethan's reckoning, yes?" He looked at Sam for an answer.

"Right again," he said.

"And to get back again, all I'd have to do is press the same button, and in another few hours – or, to me, the blink of an eye – I'd be back here, sitting in the same place, unless I had moved in the other reality?"

Samuel nodded, and uncrossed his legs. "Correctomundo," he said. Jake smiled, and said: "In that case, see you soon."

Then Jake – my clever mate Jake, the most intelligent person I knew – did the stupidest thing he'd ever done in his life.

He stared me straight in the eyes, and, as Sam and I watched in horror and disbelief, pressed the DART button deliberately and carefully.

126

Before he vanished into thin air, I heard him cry, à la Buzz Lightyear: "To infinity and beyond!"

Waiting

Sam and I sat there for a second or two, speechless. I think my jaw dropped open. The space next to me on the bed, where Jake had been sitting, was empty – I could even see the dent his buttocks had made on the duvet.

I looked at Sam. He was staring at the empty bed, too. "Oh my god," I said. "Jake!"

Sam was clearly furious, but seemed sad, too. He looked me in the eye. "Did you know he was going to do that?" he asked. He sounded like my headteacher did when he was addressing the school after an 'incident.'

I shook my head vigorously. "No, no, of course not," I said – and I hadn't. I added: "I mean, I knew he was excited about DARTing, and really keen to do it, and that he thought you may say no, but I never thought..."

Sam obviously believed me, for he just shook his head again. "Silly boy," he said. I felt ashamed. "What are we going to do?" I asked.

Sam shrugged. "Nothing we can do," he said, "except wait for him to come back." He got up and, without asking, lay down on my bed and shut his eyes. I was astonished. "What? Are you not going to go after him?" I asked.

Sam opened one eye. "And endanger my life? I-ART will be onto me quicker than I can go looking for your friend, Ethan. Anyway, Jake's only gone for the experience. I expect he'll have a quick look around the house then come straight back. To him it'll only take ten minutes, but unfortunately from our end it'll be about what?" he looked at the clock on the wall, "three hours there and three hours back, you work it out." And he shut his eyes again.

I sat on the edge of the bed and put my head in my hands. Oh Jake, why did you do this to me?

We stayed there, not speaking, for hours. I went downstairs after a while to make sure mum was still asleep – she was snoring gently – and that Lizzie wouldn't come up and disturb us. She was busy watching telly, but wanted to know what was for tea. Always thinking of her stomach, my sister – skinny as a rake, but ate like a pig.

I assured her I wouldn't let her starve, and went back upstairs to my room. Samuel was asleep – I suppose my bed was much comfier than he was used to lately. I looked at the clock. It was half past six – three and a half hours had passed since Jake disappeared, and I supposed he was probably on his way back by now. At least, I hoped so.

Half an hour later, though feeling sick with worry, I fixed a sandwich for mum and Lizzie, and made sure they were staying out of the way. Mum was awake now, and I felt it safer to tell her the visitors had left while she was asleep.

She seemed disappointed she hadn't been able to say goodbye to Sam, but happy when I said he wasn't going 'home' just yet. Little did she know how true that was!

Back upstairs, I sat on the edge of the bed and waited, one eye on the clock, the other on the space on the bed from where Jake had vanished.

When six hours had passed, Sam woke up. He didn't say anything to me, just stared at the end of the bed.

I felt terrible. Although it wasn't really my fault, if anything happened to Jake I'd never forgive myself.

We sat there, me biting my nails, which I hadn't done since I was a little kid, Samuel just staring. I was beginning to get a bit scared of him.

Ten more minutes passed, then fifteen. It was nearly half past nine when suddenly, without warning, Jake reappeared in exactly the same spot he'd left. It made me jump.

He looked exactly the same, which I suppose shouldn't have surprised me, but did, and was holding the DART in the same hand as before, finger on the DARTing button.

Before Sam or I had a chance to say anything, Jake stared wildly at me and said, in a scared little boy

131

voice I'd never heard him use before: "Ethan! Ethan! You have to do something! Your dad is going to hurt Lizzie!"

My other bedroom

At that moment, Samuel leapt to his feet and snatched the DART from Jake's hand. I thought for a second he was going to hit Jake, he looked so angry, but instead he put the DART carefully into his top pocket with the other one, and fastened it up.

Jake was saying something, but Sam wasn't listening. Instead, he looked sadly at Jake, shook his head, and left the room.

I couldn't believe this was happening. Jake was still ranting on about something, but I couldn't concentrate because Sam was heading down the stairs. I ran after him, not wanting him to go like this, not able to shout because mum thought he'd already left. "Sam!" I half-whispered. "Please!"

As he reached the front door, he turned a little and looked at me. "See you, Ethan," he said, as he left.

Slightly heartened – after all, he didn't have

anything to be angry with *me* about – I slowly went back upstairs to Jake, who was still sitting on my bed, his mobile phone in his hand, reading texts.

He looked up as I went in. He had the grace to look a bit ashamed.

"Sorry," he said, simply, and continued reading his messages. I sat down next to him on the bed, angry but relieved he was back safe. He put the phone down and gestured to it. "My dad's been phoning and texting me while I've been away," he said. "Of course, I couldn't receive them in the other reality. I'd better let him know I'm OK."

I nodded, and he phoned his dad and asked him to come and pick him up. It was late, after all. I could hear his dad on the other end, annoyed he couldn't get in touch earlier. Jake told him some tale about his phone being lost in the garden.

When he'd finished, he turned to me. "Sorry," he said again. I shrugged, still not trusting myself to say anything in case it became heated. I was still angry at him, but of course I was also keen to find out what he'd seen in the other world – and what he'd meant about dad and Lizzie.

He seemed to understand this, for he said: "I'm really sorry, Ethan, but I couldn't help myself. I didn't think Sam would let us DART at all, and I just *had* to." He paused. "I thought it might be my only chance," he went on.

I nodded, understanding. Jake was so interested in everything – science, geography, history – that he'd find it unbearable to know about these other worlds and never be allowed to go to one.

He took my silence well, and continued: "Anyway, my dad will be here in half an hour, so I have to talk fast. I need to tell you what I saw."

He shut his eyes briefly, then told me what happened: "When I pressed the button, I felt a bit tingly, and everything went black. You, Sam, the room, everything disappeared in an instant, and my head started to hurt. When my vision returned, I realised I was still in your bedroom, only it wasn't your bedroom anymore.

"I was still sitting on a bed, but the duvet was brown, not blue, and the carpet was a deep red with little grey flecks in it. I looked at the wall in front of me, and instead of your Doctor Who and Star Wars posters there were four framed pictures in a row, showing places I didn't recognise.

"To the right, your bedroom furniture had been replaced with a different, more expensive, set, in deep brown. There was a bookcase over there, with lots of books in it, and a lava lamp on the top. I couldn't see the book titles, but there was one on the bed beside me.

"Without letting go of the DART – I was scared of putting it down in case I lost it – I reached out and picked up the book. It was called The Causes of World War Three. This, of course, surprised me a little, so I turned it over and read the cover notes on the back. It seems in Samuel's world the Suez Crisis in 1956 – have you heard of that? (I nodded) – actually led to a world conflict, in which thousands of people were killed.

"Anyway, sufficiently convinced by now this was indeed a whole new, parallel world, I put the book down and listened intently. I wanted to know if anyone was in the house, as I just intended to maybe look around for ten minutes before coming back, but I didn't want to run into anyone.

"I couldn't hear anything, and so got up and looked out of the window. Outside was just as you had described it – the neat drive, some manicured plants – and there was a Mercedes car parked in the driveway. So I knew your dad was home, anyway.

"This meant I didn't dare to look round the house, so I sat down again in the same place, feeling a bit scared, I have to say. I was just debating with myself how long I should stay, when I heard voices coming up the stairs.

"At first I could only hear a man's and a boy's voice, but then there was a little girl voice, too. They seemed to be having an argument – at least, the man's voice was raised, and angry.

"I didn't want to know what they were saying, I

really didn't – getting involved is not a good idea, obviously – but I couldn't help it. They came onto the landing, and I could hear every word... Oh, Ethan."

Jake stopped, and I looked at him. He seemed to have tears in his eyes, and was obviously upset. "Go on," I said, grimly.

Jake took a deep breath, and finished his story. "The man – your dad in another world – was shouting at the boy, telling him he was lazy and stupid and wouldn't amount to anything. I think he was dragging him along, because I could hear the boy shouting 'let go' and 'you're hurting me.' The little girl was crying, and saying 'daddy don't' over and over."

Jake took another deep breath. Clearly what he had heard had been really upsetting. He went on: "The man must have pushed the boy to the floor, because I heard a thud and a cry, then he started ranting at them both, using words I couldn't possibly repeat, and threatening them with a beating if they didn't 'buck up' – his words – and 'treat him with the respect he deserved.' He said something horrible about your mum being lazy, and then the boy – he sounded like you, Ethan, only older – must have had enough, because he started shouting at his dad, telling him he was a bully and that they'd all had enough of him."

Jake stopped, and I thought that was the end of the story, but he was just gathering courage to tell me the worst bit. He looked me in the eye, and continued: "I'm sorry, Ethan, and I know this wasn't your dad, as such, but..."

I gestured for him to go on, and he did: "The man must have hit him, because I heard a smack and another thud. The little girl started crying even more, shouting 'Ivan, Ivan!' – the boy's name, I presume – and then the man said: 'Shut up, Lizzie, or you'll get the same thing in a minute.' It was then all my courage deserted me, and I'd had enough. I pressed the button and came back here."

We sat in silence for a few minutes, him reliving what he'd seen and heard, me horrified at what my family was like in another world. That boy – presumably my other dimension 'brother' – must be putting up with a lot. And poor Lizzie...

When we heard a car outside, Jake got up from the bed, said: "I have to go, it's my dad," and I followed him downstairs to the door. Showing him out, I wondered if we'd ever see Sam again, or if he'd leave that night. Jake seemed to guess what I was thinking, for he said: "Don't worry, it'll all be OK," as he left.

I wasn't too sure about that. Before I went to bed I looked in on Lizzie – she had her arms up round her head, like she used to when she was a baby, and she was snoring – and, acting on an impulse I couldn't control, went over to her bed and kissed her gently on the forehead.

As I went to sleep that night, one thing kept coming into my mind over and over again: Mum had been right to kick dad out.

Just before I fell asleep, my phone beeped – I had a text message. It was Jake. It simply said: "Cant sleep. We have 2 do something 2 help Lizzie."

An unwelcome visitor

The rest of that week I could barely contain myself. I wanted to go and see if Sam had left, but was scared of what I'd find – or not find, to be more precise. Jake couldn't come round; to be honest, I wasn't sure I wanted him to just yet. I was still angry with him for being so reckless; but he kept texting me, and rang every night. He seemed to be having trouble getting over his unsettling experience in the other reality.

Meanwhile, mum had taken to her bed again, and kept asking about Sam and when he was going to come round. I truly couldn't tell her.

I spent a lot of time with Lizzie those few days, playing games with her, taking her out for a walk, buying her sweets. I suppose I was trying to make up for being absent in another reality where she was obviously having a bad time. I know it sounds stupid, but that's how it felt.

At last I couldn't stand it anymore. I had to go and see if Sam was still there. Jake wanted to come, but I said no – I didn't think our new friend would be so happy to see him after what he'd done. As a peace offering, Jake made me promise to take Sam a tenner from him – I borrowed it out of the shopping money – so he could buy himself some beer or something.

So, the note safely in my jeans pocket, I walked down the lane towards the beach feeling a little apprehensive, to say the least. I was also carrying a plastic bag full of food and drink, 'stolen' from home again, and meant to use that as an excuse for going to see Sam.

The weather had turned a little – it was beginning to rain, and I was getting wet – but it was warm enough, and I felt that familiar pleasure as I turned onto the beach and started to crunch along the sand towards the coastguard house.

As I approached, I felt even more nervous – what if Sam was angry with me? What – even worse – if he had gone for good?

I called out his name as I went round the back of the house, softly at first then more loudly when I didn't get an answer. It seemed like no-one was at home, so I went inside the open door and, cautiously, through to the hall. The door to the living room was ajar, and I peered through, calling "Sam?" as I did. The room was empty, but Sam's things were still there, which was a good sign. I put the bag of food down by his neatly rolled-up sleeping bag – I'd brought him a camping chair to sit on, so he didn't need to sit on the floor any more.

Just as I was wondering if I should leave him a note, I was suddenly grabbed from behind by a strong pair of arms, tripped at the ankles and flung to the floor. A heavy body sat on top of me.

A gruff voice I didn't know growled in my ear: "Where is he?"

My nose an inch away from the dusty floor, my arms trapped behind me by the stranger sitting on my back, I was hardly in a position to answer, even if I had wanted to. All the air seemed to have been forced out of my lungs by the fall, and I was so squashed by the weight of the man sitting on me I couldn't take another one, but I tried.

"You're squashing me!" I said – or, at least, that's what I tried to say; barely a squeak escaped my mouth.

The man seemed to understand he was putting too much weight on me, for he sat up a little, releasing my chest from the floor. I took a deep breath in, and promptly started a coughing fit as I inhaled a load of dust.

The man tightened his grip on my arms, which were trapped behind my back, and repeated his question, a centimetre from my ear: "I said, where is he?" He sounded annoyed, but calm, and for a second I thought he was just going to snap my back and kill me. I had no idea who he was, of course, but I did know I wasn't going to tell him anything if I could help it.

"I don't know who you mean," I said, trying to sound brave. The man pulled on my arms a little harder, and it hurt. Tears came into my eyes.

"Try again, sonny," he said, "I heard you calling his name. Where is he?"

I decided there was no point in trying to play dumb, so I just told the truth: "I don't know," I squeaked. "I haven't seen him for days."

I thought he'd let me go then, but instead he pressed down on my back a bit more, and I started to yell. I knew there was no point screaming, because there'd be no-one around, but it hurt so much I needed to let off steam. At the very least I thought it might make him stop hurting me. Instead, it just seemed to annoy him more.

Too trapped to struggle, I just lay there, shouting, the man much too strong to throw off my back. I can't remember what I was yelling – I'm not ashamed to say I was scared stiff – but I do remember thinking I may never see mum and Lizzie again.

Suddenly, the man's weight was lifted off me, my arms were released and I heard a familiar voice saying angrily and deliberately: "Leave the boy alone." It was Sam.

I turned over, rubbing my arms to numb the pain, and from my position on the dusty floor saw my friend, neatly dressed in clean jeans and a sweatshirt I recognised as my dad's, pinning the man up against the wall next to the door. I was pleased to see him, of course, but a little surprised to notice he had a knife pressed up against the man's throat. Clearly, he meant business.

Without taking his eyes from the man in front of him, he said to me: "Are you OK, Ethan?" I stuttered a yes, and sat up in a crouch.

Sam had his body pressed against the man's, so he couldn't move. I studied him closely. He was a little shorter than Sam, about the same age, with the same greying, longish hair and slim but muscly build. He was wearing a neat black shirt and trousers.

His hands were by his sides, and I could see he didn't have any weapons. He started to say something, but Sam cut him short.

"I don't want to hear it, Duncan," he said. "Honestly, I didn't think hurting little boys was your style." The man – Duncan – tried to move his arms, but Sam pressed the knife a little deeper into his neck. It must have hurt, though it wasn't drawing blood yet. Sam warned him: "Don't think I wouldn't hurt you, though, because you know I would," he said.

The man sneered, which in the circumstances I thought rather unwise, but Sam laughed. He started to talk again, and I realised he was addressing me, not his prisoner. "You see, Ethan," he said, "this man has been trying to hurt me for years. So far, he's been really rubbish at it." He seemed to be trying to annoy the other man, and I think he was succeeding, if the look in his eyes was anything to go by.

By this time I think Sam must have loosened his grip a little, for the other man managed to speak up. His voice was calm, but a little gruff because of the pressure of the knife still held to his throat. "Oh Samuel," he said, "don't underestimate me. I found you yet again, and – as the Terminator so aptly said, I'll be back."

With that, he disappeared into thin air, leaving Sam

147

to stumble forward under his own weight, now pressed against nothing, and score a cut in the wallpaper with his knife.

Sam swore. Quite a bit. In fact, he used a few words I hadn't heard before – I presumed they were swear words in his reality.

After a minute or two of swearing, he turned to me, and I was surprised to see a big grin on his face. "Sorry," he said. I wasn't sure what he was sorry for – the swearing, the fact I'd seen him nearly kill someone, or the fact his acquaintance had hurt me – so I just said it was OK, and got up from the floor. My legs gave way under me – I think I must have been more scared than I was letting on – and I sat down heavily on the camp chair.

Sam rushed over. "Are you sure you're OK?" he said. "Duncan didn't hurt you, did he?" He sounded really worried, and I reassured him I was alright. He fetched me a mug of lemonade, rolled out the sleeping bag and sat down in front of me, watching me carefully.

I drank the drink, and immediately felt a lot better. Sam started to quiz me on what had happened, and I told him why I was there – I gave him the food, which he was very grateful for, and the ten pounds from Jake, which he didn't want to take, but I insisted: "I'm not taking it home again," I said, "Jake'll kill me."

Smiling, he put it in his pocket, saying he'd gladly buy himself a few bottles of beer with it. "But I haven't drunk alcohol for so long I'll probably pass out after a pint," he laughed. "And don't let Jake think it'll buy my forgiveness," he added, still smiling. "I want to let him sweat a bit longer."

He went and got himself a drink, offered me another one, which I refused, and sat down again on the floor, sipping from his mug and eyeing me carefully.

I wanted to know more about the man who'd been looking for him – Duncan – but was rather scared to ask. Thankfully, Sam must have read my mind – he was good at that – because he suddenly said: "You want to know who Duncan is, and why he's been following me, right?" I nodded. Sam sighed, crossed his legs into what I by now knew as his story-telling position, and looked me in the eye.

"He's my brother."

Duncan

"Your brother?" I was a little puzzled. I thought Sam told us he had no relatives or friends.

Sam sipped his lemonade, and grinned. "Well," he said, "my other reality brother, if you like. Duncan Harding is the alternative me, or at least one of them – I suspect there's thousands of alternatives of all of us, out there in other realities. He's the only one I've come across, and the only one I want to, thanks very much."

I thought this over for a minute, still rubbing the feeling back into my arms. "So you discovered him in another reality?" I asked.

Samuel nodded. "Yup... only we, er... we didn't exactly hit it off."

I thought about the knife pressed against his throat, and said: "I suppose not. But why is he trying to hurt you?"

Sam sighed, and shifted his position, putting down his mug. "It's a long story," he said. "But basically I found him about six years ago when I came upon a version of reality where my family was all still alive.

"You see, in my reality my parents are both dead, I never had any siblings, and my extended family's all cither dead or gone away. So I was pleased to find this one – there were my mum and dad, just like I remembered them only older, still living in the same town as we used to. I couldn't resist making contact, although of course they had no idea who I was – in their reality, as I've already explained, I couldn't possibly exist."

I nodded – I remembered you couldn't DART to a reality in which you were still there.

Sam went on: "But of course I first had to check that I had *never* existed in that reality – if another version of me had died three years ago, say, that would have been a bit of a shock for them."

I thought of the surprise the elderly couple would have had if their son, long dead, had suddenly knocked at the door, and shuddered. It didn't bear thinking about.

"So you went and said hello?" I asked.

"Yup. I pretended I was a door to door salesman. Sad, I know, but I just wanted to see them once more."

I could understand that. "So what happened?"

Sam looked at the floor. It was obviously a painful memory for him. "I managed to get inside – I can be very persuasive, you know – and they were just like my mum and dad. It nearly broke my heart to see them again. I remember asking them about their family, and they mentioned they had a son. My heart skipped a beat, because for a minute I thought they meant me. Of course they meant Duncan."

He stopped, remembering. I urged him to go on.

"So Duncan is your other reality brother, like I have a 'brother' in your reality – the one Jake and I went to?"

Sam nodded. "Duncan is like my shadow, or a mirror image – he's like me in so many ways, but totally opposite in others. After I left my other reality parents – by the way, that sort of action, seeking out your own family, is totally forbidden by I-ART, but I've never been one to keep to the rules – I discovered the son they were talking about was an agent, just like me, for their version of I-ART."

I was surprised. "So there are other realities with the same technology as yours?" I asked.

"Of course there are," said Sam. "It would be amazing if there weren't, wouldn't it? I've told you there are probably millions of alternative realities. Lots of them must have made the same discoveries as we have."

I realised what this meant. "So there must be thousands of agents out there, just jumping from reality to reality, all the time?"

Sam grinned again. "Naturally. Only it's such a small drop in the ocean you're not going to come across many in a lifetime, are you? You and Jake were really lucky."

I supposed we were. He went on: "Anyway, Duncan, it turns out, works for their I-ART. It has the same name, and for all intents and purposes is the same organisation, only their aims are not as benevolent as ours."

"What do you mean?"

"I mean they are not searching for better ways of running the planet, or a cure for malaria, or a way to feed the starving millions more easily." He paused, for effect I guess. "They're looking for better weapons."

I was shocked. "Oh," I said. "So Duncan's one of the bad guys?" Sam smiled. "Sort of. He's not evil, just doing his job... and since he discovered I existed, he's been trying to... well, let's say he doesn't really want me in the picture anymore. It's a kind of professional rivalry."

"He's after what you know?" I asked, rather cleverly, I thought.

Sam grinned. "Oh yes. Such as it is. Getting hold of another agent, but from another reality, would be a real coup – it would give them so much more information."

"How has he been following you?" I asked.

Sam shrugged. "His DART can track others, just like ours can. His must have some sort of facility for tracing reality paths which is more efficient than ours. For a short time window he can follow me when I've DARTed. So every now and again he turns up – but I always outsmart him, don't you worry."

We sat talking for a little longer, before Sam declared he was hungry and wanted some of the food I had brought. So we shared a packet of biscuits and a packet of crisps, munching in companionable silence, while I thought over what he'd said.

After another drink, I decided to broach the subject of Jake's adventure in Sam's reality. I was a bit worried Sam would be angry with him, and so at me, but he was interested in what had happened and wanted to know what he had seen.

When I got to the bit about Jake hearing 'my dad' attacking his children, he stopped eating and looked serious. I hesitated, but he told me to continue, so I did, finishing with the bit about Jake hearing their version of Lizzie being threatened.

Sam sighed, and put down a half-eaten chocolate biscuit. He looked up at me. "You can't go interfering," he said quietly.

I just looked back at him. He went on: "There are thousands of versions of Lizzie out there, many of whom are having a hard time. There are also thousands of versions of your mum, and Jake, and yourself, many of whom will be having the worst time imaginable. What are you going to do? Seek them all out and save them all, one by one?" I thought about this, but said nothing. It was kind of scary when you put it like that.

Sam added: "The one thing you learn when you become an agent is not to interfere in others' lives, because in at least one other reality, they will be doing the right thing. In countless realities your dad is a really great guy, Ethan – he's loving, and gentle, and the best dad ever. In countless others he's a monster. In millions of others he was never born.

"You can't worry yourself about what is happening elsewhere. You have to content yourself with your own version of reality – just try and get that one right, OK?"

I knew what he was saying made sense, but I couldn't shake the thought of Lizzie being hurt out of my mind. And another thing had occurred to me. In our conversation earlier, Sam had said Duncan had managed to find him because he could trace his DART path in a "short time window" – that meant Sam had to have DARTed recently.

I asked him now if he had. He looked ashamed, smiled, and then pulled something out of his back jeans pocket. It was a bundle of documents in a plain brown envelope. I asked him what it was.

"It's my passport to a new life," he said. "Literally." I looked blankly at him, so he went on: "Passport, national insurance, tax history, even a CV!"

I still must have looked blank, for he explained. "I went home, Ethan – to my reality. There's a few people I know who owe me favours, who pulled a few strings, and got me the things I needed to create a new identity in another reality. It's been done before, lots of times. I had to risk being discovered – man, I'm still good – but I needed to do it, so I can start afresh here."

I was impressed. "So that's how Duncan could find you?" I asked. Sam nodded, and went on, obviously excited: "But that's not all I went home for." And he reached into another pocket and pulled out what looked like a box of antibiotics you get from the chemist. I was puzzled again. "What are they?" I asked.

Sam blushed, and passed them to me. "I got them from another friend, in the pharmaceutical industry, who owed me another favour," he said. I read the label. It had a long, technical-sounding name I didn't recognise, but underneath in smaller writing it said: "For the treatment of Myalgic Encephalopathy (Chronic Fatigue Syndrome). Take one pill once a day with food for three months. Complete the course."

Myalgic Encephalopathy – ME – was what my mum had! I looked down at Sam, amazed. There is no cure for ME in our reality – as I told you, some doctors don't even think it's a real illness. Could this be one?

Sam just shrugged again. "I wanted your mum to be better," he said, simply.

Plotting

Sam wouldn't let me take the pills home – he wanted to give them to mum himself, so he could try and get her to take them. I had no idea how he was going to do that, nor did I ask.

As I was leaving him that day, I did cheekily ask him one more thing – how bringing some pills to hopefully cure mum was "not interfering in others' lives." He just smiled at me and said: "Hey, do as I say, not as I do, OK?"

When I told Jake on the phone later, he was astonished, and shocked to hear about Duncan. At the end of my tale, he said: "So Sam's going to stay for good, then?"

"I suppose so," I said. I didn't think he had much choice, really, but now he had some sort of identity, he could try to get a job, maybe find somewhere to live. Hopefully he'd stick around – I sort of thought he might want to. After all, we were the only friends he had.

Jake was equally amazed at the potential cure for mum. He knew as well as I did that there was no treatment, let alone cure, for ME in our reality.

"Sam must really care for your mum, Ethan," he said.

I shrugged – yeah, I know I was on the phone, but you do that, don't you? – and I think I blushed a little. "I suppose so," I said again.

"And when you care for someone," added my friend, "you go out of your way to help them, don't you?" He sounded like he was talking to a five-year-old, and I was a bit annoyed. "What are you talking about, Jake?" I said.

My friend sighed. "I think we have to help Lizzie," he said. "The other Lizzie, I mean. We have to do something."

I sighed in turn. "Yeah, that would be great, Jake," I said. "But you heard what Sam said – it made sense. You can't rescue everyone. And anyway, he'll never let us DART again – you made sure of that." I couldn't help taking a swipe at his actions.

"Ouch," he said in response.

Just then Lizzie shouted from outside the bedroom door: "Ethan?" I told Jake to hang on a second, and opened the door to her. She was still dressed in her pyjamas, having not bothered to get dressed all day, and had a tray in her arms. On it was a plate of crackers with cheese, a mug of juice and a cup cake. She offered it to me. "Here you go, Ethan," she said, "I made you some tea."

I took the tray, putting my mobile phone down on the bed to do so, and thanked her. She looked pleased. "I just wanted to do something for you," she said sweetly, "because you're always doing things for me and mum." And with that she ran off to her room, skipping down the corridor.

I put the tray down on the bed and picked up the phone.

Jake had heard what had gone on. "She's very sweet, isn't she?" he said. I nodded – yeah, yeah, I was

163

on the phone, I know – and grunted a yes. Jake went on: "You see, Ethan, I think it's important to help those we love, even if we can only do it once. Better to save one person's life than none at all, yeah?"

I nodded again, worried now. "OK," I said, "what's the plan?"

....

It took Jake and I a week or so to come up with an idea of what we were going to do. We kept arguing about the finer points, and I don't think we ever really came up with a great plan, but the gist of it was we were going to steal – well, borrow – one of Sam's DARTs while he was asleep or drunk, and go and talk to my other reality brother, Ivan, about how he must protect his sister.

I had no idea whatsoever how we were going to get Sam into the necessary state, or what we were going to say to Ivan if we managed to get to see him. There were so many unknowables – who would be in the house at the time we DARTed, whether anyone would let us in the house, whether Ivan would let us talk to him, what we were actually going to say to him, etc, etc – that in the end we gave up trying to make plans and decided we'd just go ahead if we got the chance.

"After all," said Jake, "we know we can just DART home again at the first sign of danger. As long as we stay together, we'll be safe whatever happens." Yeah, yeah.

What we did decide on was that we'd DART from outside the house, so we could knock at the door (rather than appear from nowhere inside it) and pretend to be friends of Ivan's if anyone else opened it. If Ivan answered, we had some story about being a friend of a friend ready, in order to get to talk to him. Another thing we agreed on was, if my 'dad' was home (we'd see his car) we'd DART home straight away, and not take the risk. Neither Jake nor I wanted to see or hear him again.

But the question still remained about when we were going to do it, and how we'd get hold of the

DART. Fortunately, Sam himself answered these questions for us.

He had been coming round more and more often recently – he was becoming a regular visitor now. At first he'd come to visit mum, and stay in her room for hours on end, talking to her. I know he had persuaded her to take the pills – how I didn't know – and that she was very pleased when he came and upset when he left.

Lizzie, too, was pleased to see him at the door, and the two of them spent some time together, playing card games Sam taught her and watching rubbish TV. Sam seemed fascinated by kids' telly (he said they didn't have kids' channels in his reality), and would laugh like a drain at some of the funnier ones. Mum even joined them on the sofa a few times.

It was during one of his visits that he unwittingly provided Jake and I with the ideal chance to carry out what we were by now calling Operation Lizzie. Unimaginative, I know, but we liked the idea of being secret agents on a mission.

Sam was helping me get the tea ready for us all – Jake was there, too. I think it was a Sunday, because we were making a roast. Mum had helped prepare the veg, but was now resting in her bedroom, while Sam and I were putting the finishing touches to the gravy and potatoes. I had asked Sam if he thought mum was getting any better, and he replied he thought so, yes, then he mentioned it was her birthday the following week.

"I know," I said, stirring the gravy. "I've already got her a card, and I've been saving all month so I've got a few pounds to buy her something."

Sam smiled. "You're a good son, Ethan," he said. I blushed. He went on: "I was thinking... feel free to say no, but I thought we could throw a little party for her? You know, an old-fashioned one, with balloons, a cake... jelly and ice cream..."

I laughed. "Always thinking of your stomach, aren't you?" I said. Sam laughed too. "Naturally," he said. "But what do you think? I could get some food and maybe a bottle of wine for me and your mum –

you know I'm getting benefits now I have an identity, so I'm feeling a bit flush at the moment." That was true, alright. Sam had risen from being literally penniless to being on the dole – and it must have felt like he'd won the lottery. He could now afford to eat and buy stuff, and was spending lots of time in the library looking for a job. I was sure he'd get one soon – his CV, made up as it was, was pretty impressive!

Anyway, I agreed a party would be a good idea – her birthday was the following Saturday, and we decided we'd tell mum and not make it a surprise, which might be too much for her. Jake would be invited, of course, and Lizzie's best friend Sarah, who lives nearby, although we didn't have any other family and mum didn't really have any friends anymore.

So it would just be the usual crowd, having a special lunch – only with added cake. Sounded good to me – and for more than one reason. If Sam was in a party mood, and drinking alcohol, I reasoned maybe we'd be able to get a DART away from him and sneak out for a few hours. Make that six.

I told Jake later that day, when the adults had retired to the lounge and Lizzie was in her room. He was very excited, but I didn't anticipate his next question: "Have you got any vodka in the house?"

"You what?" "Vodka – you know, it's a clear alcohol." "I know what it is, Jake," I said.

"Well?"

I didn't know – we had a cupboard in the kitchen with old bottles of alcohol in, left over from when my dad had left. Mum didn't usually drink, but I thought dad may have left a couple of bottles of whisky. I told Jake I'd look later, and asked him why he wanted some – surely he wasn't thinking of having any?

"No, you daft sod," he said, rather cruelly, I thought. "Vodka is virtually tasteless, so you can add it to other drinks, like orange juice, without anyone knowing. We could use it to get Sam a bit tipsy early on – don't forget, we need lots of time to carry out Operation Lizzie successfully. It'll take us six hours just travelling there and back."

I nodded. Yes, I'd been worrying about that. Even

if we only spent an hour there, that meant a whopping seven hours away from everyone – how on earth were we going to get away with that?

Mum's party

The day of the party came quickly. It was near the end of August, and for a change the sun was shining, so we decided to make it a barbecue. Sam was to bring some burgers and sausages, while I would provide the buns, salad, dressings etc.

Lizzie and her friend made some cakes from a packet, and iced them very messily on the kitchen worktop, while Jake and I laid the food out on the table. We had already blown up some balloons and arranged mum's birthday cake – complete with token candles – in the centre.

Mum stood in the doorway and supervised. She was certainly feeling better – she'd been out of bed for the best part of a week, and wasn't getting as tired as usual. I noticed she had her best jeans and top on, and had even managed to wash and straighten her hair.

Sam arrived just before 11 with a card and bunch

of flowers for mum, the food, a couple of disposable barbecues, two bottles of wine and a four-pack of beer. He set about lighting the barbecues – "They always take forever to get up to the right temperature," he said – while Jake and I poured some drinks for everyone and helped mum open her presents. Lizzie and I got her a pretty silver bracelet, while Jake and his family had bought her a DVD of her favourite TV comedy show. She was very pleased.

Jake grabbed me in the hall as I was on the way to put mum's cards on the mantelpiece for her.

"Did he bring them?" he asked.

"Bring what?" I asked back.

Jake looked at me as if I was an idiot, which I suppose I was. "The DARTs!" he said, in a loud whisper I thought next door must have heard.

I shushed him, and pointed at Sam's jacket, which was hanging on the bottom of the banister. "He never goes anywhere without them, so I expect they're in his pocket," I said, rather impatiently. I was nervous as hell. I didn't want to do this at all – I'd much rather just enjoy the party. But I knew Jake was determined to carry out the mission whether I went or not, and felt I should really help him – Lizzie was *my* sister, after all.

So I stood in the hall, keeping watch, while Jake felt in Sam's pockets for the DARTs. Being hard and round, they were easy to feel, and Jake smiled and nodded after just a few seconds. Part of me was relieved, but my stomach seemed to fall down to my shoes as I realised what that meant. There was no going back now.

Jake headed back to the kitchen like a man on a mission – which he was, of course – and poured Sam a large glass of wine.

....

The party was a resounding success. The food was great (Sam had obviously had plenty of practice at cooking rough) and mum enjoyed herself immensely.

After we'd all eaten, we played party games for a while, feeling like little kids but having fun. Sam was expert at Twister, although he swore he'd never played it before, and then Lizzie and Sarah entertained us all with a song and dance routine they'd made up especially. It was dreadful, but we applauded them nonetheless.

Finally, Sam emerged from the kitchen with the cake, all 12 candles burning away, and we sang happy birthday while mum blew them out. Tearfully, she told us all it was the best birthday she'd had in a long time, and I know it wasn't just the wine talking. She hugged everyone, then went into the house for a rest.

Jake obviously thought it was time to get moving – I was hoping it would get too late to do anything, but it seemed fate was on his side, not mine.

Lizzie and Sarah went up to her bedroom to play, and Sam went into the lounge to watch TV while mum rested. He'd already had two glasses of wine and a bottle of beer, and was obviously a bit tipsy. When Jake went in with another bottle of beer (we had earlier found out there was no vodka, alas), he greeted him with a cheery: "Jakey boy, come and give your uncle Sam a big hug!" Jake passed him the beer, but ignored the plea for a cuddle and instead said, amused: "I thought we were cousins."

Sam looked a bit confused. "Oh yeah," he said. "I forgot." He grinned, and pointed at the TV, which was showing a kids' history programme.

"I sooooo love your reality," he said. Jake smirked, pleased at the way this was going. Sam went on: "Your TV is brilliant. Brilliant! And you don't have to pay for it!" Jake looked briefly at the television, and said: "Well, we do have to buy a TV licence."

Sam waved a hand in his direction, and took a swig from the beer bottle. "Pah!" he said. "A mere pittance. In my reality we have to pay a fortune for just 12 channels – imagine that!

He took another swig, and added: "*And* they're all rubbish!"

Jake laughed, and turned to look at me, anxiously standing in the doorway. "Sam," he said. Sam looked at him, a little short-sightedly, as if he couldn't focus properly.

"Yes, Jakey boy?" "Ethan and I are just going out for a bit. A friend of mine lives three roads away and he texted to say he has a new computer game we can try out. You'll be OK on your own for a few hours, won't you?"

This was new. A stroke of genius on Jake's part, I thought – at least it would buy us some time out of the house. Sam nodded vigorously. "Of course, old chap," he said. "The party's winding down now, anyway..." Winding down? I think it had all but fizzled out. "...Heather's happy as Barry, and I'll just put my feet up and enjoy the ambience."

So speaking, he did as he said and put his feet up on the sofa. As we left, I think I saw his eyes closing.

"He'll be asleep for hours," said Jake, as we headed down the hall. As we reached the foot of the stairs, I said I'd have to let Lizzie know we were going out, too, and went up to tell her while Jake felt in Sam's pocket for a DART. In some strange way, I didn't want to see him taking it. As we headed to the door, Jake stopped me. "Leave your mobile behind," he whispered.

"What? Why?" "It won't work in another reality, you know that – and if they see you've left it behind 'by mistake', and don't know exactly where you've gone, they'll just assume you're having too much fun to realise the time, and won't panic about you being gone for hours."

This made sense. Jake had been busy making plans after all, it seemed. I left my phone on the glass table in the hall, where I sometimes placed it when I was in the house. That would be convincing.

"But what if they try to ring *you*?" I asked. "Your mobile number's in the address book."

Jake had thought of that, too. "I can say mine is broken – they'll believe that, but wouldn't believe two of them being out of action."

OK. I had no other excuses. It was time to carry out Operation Lizzie.

Operation Lizzie

We walked out of the door and down the drive to the gate, round the corner behind the wall – and stopped. Out of sight of the house, we felt it was safe to DART, and we wanted to do it as soon as we could so we would take as little time as possible.

After looking up and down the street to make sure no-one was watching, we stood close together, Jake held my hand – yes, I did feel stupid – and with the other hand pressed the DART button. It was in my mind to call it off, even now, but it was too late. Jake said: "Geronimo!" and the world went blank.

When I opened my eyes Jake, thankfully, was still in front of me, still holding my hand – I snatched it away – and looking dazed. I shook my head to clear it, and Jake did the same. "Wow," he whispered. "That is like being hit over the head with a sledgehammer."

I didn't have time to agree. Quickly, he put the

DART in the top pocket of his denim jacket, and buttoned it up safely. "Let's do it," he said, and we walked up the driveway of my suddenly transformed house. I was a bit disappointed to see there was no car in the driveway – indicating my 'dad' wasn't in – as it would have meant us giving up and going home, something I was desperate to do just now.

My heart beating hard in my chest, I followed Jake up the drive towards the hideous brown door I remembered crying at last time I was here. Starting to panic, I realised I just had to focus on the job in hand, let Jake do most of the talking, and get this over with as quickly as possible.

Jake seemed to be leading this mission, anyway – he seemed very cool and collected. To be honest, I was very happy just to tag along.

We went up to the door and Jake pressed the bell. We could hear it outside – it was one of those awful musical ones that played an embarrassing tune, but I didn't recognise it. We waited.

A minute later, Jake pressed the bell again, but I

was hoping no-one was in.

Unfortunately, I was wrong. Suddenly the door opened, and Lizzie stood there. She was wearing a dress I didn't recognise, and was holding a can of Coke in her hand (I never let her drink fizzy drinks – it's one of our rules) but it was Lizzie in every other aspect, down to the way she had her hair. "Yes?" she said, in Lizzie's voice.

I almost gasped out loud, it was so spooky, but Jake spoke over me: "Hi," he said calmly. "We're friends of Ivan's. Can we come in?"

'Lizzie' shrugged, and opened the door further. "He's in his room," she said.

Jake and I went in, me trying not to stare at Lizzie too much – she was exactly the same, it was just too weird – and climbed the stairs. They were in the same place as ours, but had a different bannister and carpet, I noticed. Going up the wall were a series of school photos of this Lizzie and her brother at different ages, getting older as we ascended. It was so strange I began to feel oddly disconnected to the whole event, like you do in dreams. Surely I would wake up soon?

No such luck. We got to the top of the stairs and Jake, of course, already knew which bedroom to head for – Ivan's was the same as mine. He knocked gently on the door, saying: "Ivan?"

A second or two later a boy opened the door to 'my' bedroom. I stared at him, shocked. He was taller than me, obviously a year or two older, and wearing glasses, but otherwise almost the same as me, with the same eyes and hair and the same unfortunate nose. He looked at me, and I saw a frown cross his face, then stared at Jake, who was standing slightly in front of me.

"Who are you?" he asked, not unreasonably, I thought. He sounded confused, not frightened. Jake smiled, and held out his hand for the boy to shake. "I'm Jake," he said, "and this here is my good friend Ethan. We've come to talk to you about something important. May we have a few minutes of your time?"

Ivan looked stupidly at Jake's hand, then back at his face. "How did you get in?" he asked, then answered his own question: "I suppose Lizzie let you in, did she?" Jake nodded, and put his hand back by his side. My doppelganger went on: "She's so trusting, she'll let anyone in – last week it was the Jehovah's Witnesses. Hah!" he laughed, and the tension eased a little. At least he wasn't going to throw us out – not yet, anyway.

Jake took advantage of his good mood, by asking again if we could talk to him for a minute.

He seemed confused, of course, but he shrugged and opened the bedroom door wider so we could go in.

"Who are you again?" he asked, as we sat on the bed. I looked around, and saw everything as Jake had described it after his brief but eventful visit here. There was the bookcase with a lava lamp on top, there were the framed pictures on the wall. Everywhere was neat and tidy – so unlike my own room.

Jake told him again what our names were, and he nodded, then said: "I mean, who *are* you?"

I decided to stay quiet on this one – how on earth

could I explain who I really was? – but thankfully Jake seemed to have it all planned out. "Who we are is not really important just now," he said. "What *is* important is that you listen to what we have to say."

Ivan was obviously a little taken aback by this, but he came and stood in front of us and leant back against the wall, putting his hands in his jeans pockets. "I'm listening," he said.

Jake sat forward on the bed, his hand unconsciously fingering the outline of the DART in his top pocket. I expect it reassured him to know it was still there.

"This will probably come as a shock to you," said Jake, in a serious tone, "but we know your dad hits you, and we know he threatens your sister. We've come here especially to tell you the situation will only get worse if you let it, and to encourage you to do something about it now, before it's too late." Blimey, Jake certainly believes in getting to the point, I thought.

Ivan's reaction to this was revealing. I watched as

his face at first expressed surprise, then annoyance, then anger, all in the space of a few seconds. I knew, before he spoke, what he was going to say.

"How dare you!" he shouted. Jake physically jumped, it was so loud. "I have no idea what you're talking about. Who put you up to this? My dad is a wonderful man and a great father, and I won't hear a word said against him. Now get out of my bedroom." With that, he took his hands out of his pockets and opened the door again.

Well, I had had a feeling this wasn't going to go very well, but I hadn't expected to be thrown out quite so quickly. Jake, however, wasn't going to give up that easily. He smiled, waved a hand in the vague direction of the door, and carried on talking: "There's no use denying it," he said. "We know all about it. For reasons we can't go into, it's rather close to our hearts, and we've come a long way to warn you to do something about it." he paused. "For Lizzie's sake," he added, playing his trump card.

Ivan was still standing there, holding the door

open, but now he looked ashamed, not angry, and I realised his eyes were filling up with tears. I felt so sorry for him – this was essentially the life I could have lived, had mum not stood up to dad.

There was a silence, and I realised Ivan was now staring at me intently. I looked him in the eye but decided to remain quiet. It was him, after all, who had to make his own fate.

His hand fell away from the door, and he said to me: "You look familiar. Do I know you from somewhere?"

I was half tempted to say: "The mirror, maybe?" but didn't. I shrugged instead, not trusting myself to say anything. Jake took advantage of the situation – Ivan had, for the moment at least, forgotten about throwing us out – and went on: "Look, we don't have a lot of time. All we need is for you to promise you'll do something to stop your dad being such a bully, then we'll leave you in peace for the rest of your life."

Ivan looked at him, confused again. All pretence gone, he said: "And what do you suggest I do, strange boy? He's been bullying us all our lives, why would he stop now just because I ask him to?"

I don't think Jake had thought of this, really – in fact, I hadn't, either. Just how does a kid stop their parent from being abusive when it's clearly in their nature to be so? Tell the authorities and risk being put into care? Tell the police and risk a parent being put into prison? How, exactly? I was so glad my mum had made the decision for me.

Jake was now stumped for words, and Ivan seemed to be on the verge of throwing us out again – his hand was holding the edge of the door, like it was a means of escape for him. I decided to break the awkward silence, and what came out was not planned, but came from the heart.

"Ivan," I said. He looked at me, and I saw tears in his eyes again. I didn't think he should be ashamed of them. "I know this is hard for you – believe me, I know. And I know you think we've no right to come here and tell you how to run your life, and in a way you're right. But we've really only come to make you see that, now you're old enough to stand up to bullies, you really have to do so, for your own and your family's sake. You have to do something to help Lizzie before it's too late."

There. I'd said it. Now I thought we could go with clear consciences. We'd done our best – now it was up to Ivan to do the rest. We had our own realities to cope with.

Ivan was about to say something, when there came the sound of a key in the front door.

'Dad'

All three of us turned to look at the bedroom door. I saw fear on Ivan's face, and again felt sorry for him – imagine feeling fear, not joy, at the sound of a parent's key in the lock. Quickly, Jake said: "Is that your dad?" Ivan looked at us. "It'll be him and mum," he said. "He took mum out for a drive for her birthday. We're all going out for tea."

Of course, I forgot it would be Ivan's mum's birthday, too. Damn. We'd have to go. Jake opened his top pocket, took the DART out and held it securely in his palm. Then he turned to Ivan. "We have to go. Show us out," he said. "And if they ask, we're just friends of a friend, OK?" Jake, of course, didn't want to DART in front of anyone.

Ivan looked confused and annoyed at the same time. "Hang on," he said, "I still want to know who you are.

"And what's that?" He pointed at Jake's closed fist.

"Never mind," said Jake. "It doesn't matter. Really, we have to go." I think he was beginning to panic, and a minute later I understood why, as we heard footsteps coming up the stairs, and a man's raised voice. It was my 'dad' – and he didn't sound happy.

Ivan looked fearfully at the door, and a second later my other reality dad – I'd seen him before, but was still taken aback at the sight – burst through into the bedroom. He was looking the other way, shouting angrily at someone following him: "I bother to take you out, and this is all I get – moan, moan, moan all day long. Jesus, woman, why on earth do I bother? I suppose that present will go back to the shop, too. Well, you should have told me your size before I spent the money. And don't just stand there – go and put the tea on, I'm starving."

I heard my other reality mum protesting – she must have said something about going out for a meal, because 'dad' shouted back: "You're kidding, aren't

189

you? I've spent enough money on you for one day, just be thankful for what you get. I don't know, no-one in this house appreciates me at all..." he turned to look into his son's bedroom, and saw us all standing there. "Who are you?" he barked.

Before we could answer, he turned to Ivan. "I thought I told you not to invite people round without asking. I suppose because we were out you thought you could get away with it, did you?" Ivan just looked at him. He turned to us. "Well, I'm waiting, who are you?"

I was so angry – at the way he'd just spoken to 'mum', for a start – that I didn't trust myself to speak. Jake, however, seemed to find his voice again, for he took a step forward, held out his hand and said: "So nice to meet you, Mr Jones. I'm Jake, and this is Ethan." The man ignored his hand, but Jake went on anyway: "We're friends of your son... I'm afraid we arrived unannounced. We were just leaving – we'll not trouble you any longer." And with that, he headed for the door, saying "come on, Ethan" to me.

Unfortunately 'other dad' was not in a nice mood. He stood in the doorway, blocking the way. He wasn't going to let this one pass without an argument.

"I don't recognise you from school," he said to Jake.

"Er... no, we go to a different school," replied my friend.

"Which one?"

Jake obviously couldn't think fast enough. His mouth sort of flapped open while his brain tried to think of a plausible answer, but this time at least his brain failed him. The man in the doorway came into the room, and shut the door behind him. It didn't look like we'd be leaving without explaining ourselves.

Ivan, standing beside his dad but looking like he'd rather be anywhere else in the world, started to say something, but his dad cut him short. "What have you been telling them, boy?" he asked of his son.

Ivan shook his head violently. "I don't even know them, dad," he said. Oh, thanks, 'brother,' I thought. He went on: "They just arrived at the door – Lizzie let them in." As soon as he said this, he must have realised he'd now got his sister into trouble, for he started to backtrack: "I mean, they barged inside and..." But it was too late. Other reality dad – I would call him bad dad, but my one wasn't that much better – yelled: "Elizabeth! Get in here now!"

Oh dear God, I thought, this is getting from bad to worse. I looked at Jake, and could see he was lost for ideas as to how to get out of this place and back home without having to disappear in front of everyone. Right now, the thought of just vanishing was beginning to look better and better.

We waited in silence – what could we say? – for a whole minute before the door opened and in came Lizzie. My heart sank. She looked scared to death.

"Yes, daddy?" she said.

Her father towered over her in a threatening way. He looked like a lion about to devour his prey, and I swear if he'd tried to lay one hand on her I'd have stopped him myself.

Fortunately I didn't have to. Just at that moment

192

there was a terrible scream from downstairs – my other reality mum was shouting something. She sounded terrified. All of us looked puzzled. I looked questioningly at Jake, who shrugged and grabbed my arm with his free hand – the other one, I saw, was still wrapped tightly round the DART.

Then suddenly all was chaos. Lizzie, still stood in the doorway, was flung roughly to one side as a man entered the room. Lizzie screamed, Ivan shouted something and Jake and I backed away towards the other side of the room.

The man had a gun.

He pointed it now in turn at everyone in the room, and part of me, through my terror, was a little pleased to see Ivan's dad back away in fright, a scared look on his face.

As everyone fell quiet, stunned into silence, the man spoke. "Where is Samuel?" he said – and suddenly I recognised him, although last time I saw him he had spent most of the time pinning me to the floor. It was Duncan.

At gunpoint

Duncan looked at us all, cowering in front of him. His eyes fell on me and his eyebrows raised in surprise, and he smiled. "Ah," he said. "I suppose you're here without him, are you? Taking a little trip to another reality for fun is really not advisable when you don't know what you're doing."

I stared at him. Without Samuel here to help us, we were really in danger – from all sides, it seemed. I had no idea what to say in order to save us.

Ivan's dad found his voice. "Who on earth are you, and what are you doing in my house?" he said. Although his voice was raised, he was shouting a lot quieter than when he spoke to his family, I noticed – no doubt the presence of a gun made him less of a bully.

Duncan turned the gun on dad, who visibly shrank at the sight. "I have no business with you," he said, dismissively. "It's Samuel Harding I'm after. But in his absence I suppose I'll take second best – a DART from another reality is a bonus. We can learn a lot from that." And he turned back to me.

"Give me the DART," he said, coolly.

I glanced at Jake. Of course, Duncan didn't know Jake, so probably assumed he belonged to this reality. Jake tightened his grip on the DART in his fist – he'd let go of my arm when the gunman burst into the room, so couldn't DART home without going alone. I knew he wouldn't do that, so took a step towards him. Hopefully I'd get close enough to hold onto him.

"I don't have it," I replied, truthfully, holding my hands out in front of me, palms upwards.

Duncan looked at them, then at Jake. He obviously wasn't as daft as I thought – maybe he'd seen my anxious look in Jake's direction, because he pointed the gun at Jake instead. "OK boy," he said to him. "Give me the DART, and don't mess me about or I'll shoot the girl."

I didn't know if he was bluffing or not, but Jake

wasn't taking any chances. He held out his hand and opened his fist, revealing Sam's DART. Duncan took a step forward and snatched it from him with his free hand, then put it deep into his jacket pocket.

"Thanks, sonny," he said, and my heart seemed to sink into my knees. Bye bye home, I thought. That was our only way of ever going back.

I thought at least that would be the end of the gun threat – that Duncan would disappear as quickly as he had arrived – but it was not to be. He turned the gun back to me: "Now," he said, "tell me where Samuel is."

I looked at him stupidly. "He's back in our reality," I said, deciding not to tell lies to a man with a gun in his hand.

"I guessed that, dumbo," said Duncan, "I mean where can I find him at this precise moment. You must know, because you have his DART – unless you stole it from him, of course. And you're such nice little boys you wouldn't do a thing like that, would you?"

I must have looked ashamed, because I didn't need

196

to answer. He knew. He smiled at me, and waved the gun around a bit. "Oh come on, this is getting boring. Don't worry, I'll be able to trace his DART back to your home anyway, so I'll catch up with him soon enough."

And he turned towards the bedroom door to leave. As he did so, my other reality dad did the stupidest thing he'd probably ever done. He grabbed Duncan by the shoulders – he was a bit taller, and quite a bit heavier – and yanked him to the ground in a tackle.

Lizzie screamed again, and ran out of the bedroom door. Duncan yelled and fell backwards onto the ground, with 'dad' on top of him, trying to prise the gun away from his hand. Jake and I looked at each other in anguish, but couldn't do anything without recovering Sam's DART.

Ivan, on the other hand, had seen enough. Crying "Dad!" he launched himself forward, towards the grappling men, and tried to help his dad get hold of the weapon. I shouted "No!" But it was too late. Suddenly – inevitably, it seemed – the gun went off.

There was a huge, ear-splitting bang, and when I could bear to look I saw Ivan staggering against the wall, clutching at his left side, blood beginning to spurt between his fingers.

Everything seemed to happen at once. Ivan slumped to the floor, his face grey and shocked, a wound covered by his hands, blood spilling onto the carpet. 'Dad' dropped to his side, screaming his son's name over and over. I think he was crying.

Duncan was lying on the floor, gun still in his hand, shouting: "I didn't mean it! It was an accident! You shouldn't have done that!" He looked really upset – from the way he was acting, I don't expect he had shot anyone before.

Jake and I, meanwhile, had both dropped to the floor behind Ivan's bed when the gun went off, in a reflex action to save our lives. We were crouched there, looking dumbly over the edge of the bed, and I was vaguely aware of someone shouting "Get an ambulance" – I'm not sure who it was, but it didn't matter, anyway – because immediately there was the sound of approaching sirens. Surely they couldn't have got here so soon? The gun had only just gone off!

Duncan got up off the floor, and seemed unsure what to do. He got a DART out of his pocket, and held it in one hand, the gun still in the other, though it was by now pointed at the floor. He looked at it as if he hadn't seen one before. I think he was still shocked at what had happened. As Samuel had said, he wasn't a bad man, just doing his job.

And then, just when I was thinking this couldn't get any more confused, there was a flash of light in the middle of the room, and Samuel appeared – ZAP – from out of nowhere.

I wouldn't have been more shocked if a shark had suddenly leapt through the window. Sam, however, showed just how good an agent he was by quickly and calmly assessing the situation, looking around him at Jake and I behind the bed, Duncan with a gun, Ivan wounded and his dad trying to stop the flow of blood.

Duncan, obviously believing this was not a good time to confront Samuel, threw his gun to the floor and started fiddling frantically with his DART.

Quick as a flash, Sam picked up the gun and turned it on Duncan. "I suppose you're responsible for this mess," he said to his other reality brother.

Duncan was still fiddling with his DART, and said nothing. I expect he wanted to leave the mess behind for someone else to sort out. Jake, aware he may leave any time soon, suddenly shouted: "Sam! He's got your DART!"

Sam raised his eyebrows, and then the gun, until it was pointing directly at Duncan's head. "Give me my DART," he said coldly, "and I will let you go with your brains still in your head."

Duncan looked him in the eye, and saw he meant it. He reached into his pocket, took out the other DART, and handed it to Samuel, who nodded his thanks. Then he smiled, looked at Jake and I as if he wanted to remember our faces, and pressed the button on his DART. He vanished.

Immediately, Sam dropped the gun on the floor, and raced over to where Ivan was lying. He brushed 'dad' to one side – the former bully was babbling incoherently now, having just seen one man appear and another man disappear in front of his eyes – and examined Ivan. He felt his forehead, looked in his eyes, took his pulse, then gingerly opened Ivan's fingers to see how bad the wound was.

"You'll be OK, kid," he said after a minute or two. "You're very lucky, the bullet just scraped past you – see, it went into the bookcase over there.

"But don't go tackling gunmen again, alright?" I looked at the bookcase, and saw a hole in its side where the bullet must have gone. Oh god, I thought, that could have hit any of us.

Ivan managed a faint smile, although he looked scared to death. The sirens had, meanwhile, got very loud and then stopped. Sam went to the window and looked out.

"There's police outside. I think they're armed," he said. Quickly, he turned to Jake and I. "Come here," he said. "We'd better go before we get into trouble."

We didn't need any more encouraging, came out

from behind the bed and stood next to our friend, who told us to grab hold of an arm each.

Before he pressed the button to get us home, he turned deliberately to my other reality dad, who was still babbling like a baby, and said: "Tell them you interrupted a robbery, and the gunman fled before they got here.

"If you tell them what really happened, they'll put you in a madhouse."

He paused, looked at the DART, then turned back. "Oh," he said, "one more thing. If I hear you've so much as raised your voice at your wife or children one more time, I'll be back." And with that, he pressed the button and all three of us vanished from the room.

Explanations

It seemed like seconds, but of course it was actually hours, before we opened our eyes again – to see mum and Lizzie sitting on my bed.

Mum immediately jumped up, ran towards us shouting "Ethan! Oh thank goodness." She hugged me roughly, then grabbed Jake and finally Sam in a bear hug. He hugged her back, saying: "It's OK, Heather, they're fine. Everything's going to be fine."

Lizzie, meanwhile, was staring goggle-eyed at all three of us. Her mouth was slightly open, as if she was going to say something, but I expect she was just shocked to see us appear in the middle of the room. I had no idea what mum thought – but I soon found out.

As soon as she'd hugged everyone, she stood back and started on me. "Just what on earth were you two doing?" she shouted. "I've never been so scared in all my life! We've been sitting here for hours, thinking you were dead or worse. How could you do that to us?"

I opened my mouth to make excuses, but shut it again when I realised there weren't any, really. Anyway, she hadn't finished: "If Lizzie hadn't told Sam she'd seen you disappear, I don't know what would have happened!"

Samuel shushed her, saying: "It's OK, Heather, the boys are safe – we're all safe. Let's all go and have a nice cup of tea, shall we?"

As we headed towards the bedroom door, me half expecting to see 'dad' or a bleeding Ivan in the doorway, Jake piped up: "How did Lizzie see us?" But Sam shushed him, too, saying: "We'll compare notes in the kitchen over a hot cup of tea."

....

An hour later – after two cups of tea and a Jammie Dodger each – we were all calm again. Lizzie had explained how, suspicious at my behaviour, she had listened in when Jake told me to leave my phone behind, so had gone to look out of my bedroom window to see where we were going – and had been not a little surprised to see our heads both disappear into thin air behind the garden wall.

Not knowing what had happened, or what to do, she had first sent her friend home, saying she was feeling ill, then gone to tell Samuel – she'd apparently had to wake him up first. Sam had suspected at once, of course, where we'd gone, had sobered up pretty quickly, and had followed us almost straight away using his other DART, thinking my bedroom would be the best place to appear – guessing, correctly, that we had gone to talk to Ivan.

Mum, evidently, had known for some time who Sam is and where he comes from. Those long talks in her bedroom had been Sam convincing her his story was true – he wanted to tell her the truth, he said, because he had become very fond of us all and didn't want to begin a relationship on the basis of a lie. Plus it had been the only way to get her to take the tablets she needed to make her better.

I was astonished mum hadn't said anything sooner – but then I remembered how well she kept secrets. "But no more," she said, tears in her eyes, "no more secrets." I hugged her and made another cup of tea.

When she and Lizzie heard about the shooting in the other reality, mum gasped and Lizzie put her hand over her mouth. But Sam reassured them: "He'll be fine, I promise," he said. "I did first aid training in the Army *and* in the agency, and I can tell if a wound is life-threatening. He'll be in pain for a while, but he'll live."

"But how did the police get there so soon?" I asked. Jake knew the answer to this one: "We heard your mum – sorry, I mean Ivan's mum – scream when Duncan arrived, remember?" he said. "She must have let him in, and I'm sure most people, if they see someone barge into their house with a gun, will call the police if they can."

And when Jake told mum and Lizzie what Sam had said to 'dad' before we left, mum smiled grimly. "I expect he'll think twice before he acts next time," she said. And, recalling his terrified face, I had to agree with her.

It was no thanks to us, really, but somehow I think we'd accomplished our mission.

Lizzie – at least, that one – would be OK.

Big school

On the first day of secondary school, when everyone's excited, disorientated and a bit frightened, Jake and I were talking to some kids from another primary school when Sean Roberts – my arch enemy, if you like – came across with his gang of idiots.

"What you doing talking to those losers?" he asked the new kids, pushing his way into the conversation with his usual charm.

He stood right in front of me – I noticed he'd grown a few centimetres since July, and not just in height – and poked my chest with one chubby finger.

"Oi, Ethan, Ethan, Ethan Jones, his mum's nothing more than a bag of bones," he sang to my chin – he never looked me in the face, I noticed.

Usually, this is the point where his gang would wade in, steal my bags and stamp on my school books, but not this time – this time I decided to do something to change this reality, and maybe a few others at the same time.

Immediately, I pushed him, hard, in the chest. He went stumbling backwards, tripped over his own small feet and landed – thump – in the dust of the playground. Everyone else, except me, laughed.

Oh no, this wasn't funny. This was deadly serious.

I took two steps forward, stood looking down at his bewildered face – his victim had never stood up to him before – and said in a clear voice: "I suggest you find another kid to bully, Roberts.

"I'm not the same child you knew in primary school. Now get up, leave us be, and take your cronies with you."

Amazingly, he did as I told him. His friends were still laughing at him even as they left.

Later that morning, Jake and I were alone, walking from one lesson to another, talking about the new school, teachers, etc – and about how my life would change when Sam moved in the following week.

"Mum says he's not replacing dad, but I laughed

209

and said I wish he would," I said.

"And how's your mum now?" asked Jake. He hadn't been around for a week or so.

"Oh, she's a lot better, thanks," I said. "She even managed to make tea a couple of days ago. It's amazing, really."

Jake smiled. "Well, I expect all our lives are just going to be normal from now on, hey?" he asked.

I moved my bag of books from one shoulder to the other – man, they made you read a lot in this school – and grinned.

"Maybe not," I replied. "Sam told me last night that the DART Duncan gave him was not his, after all."

Jake stopped dead in the middle of the corridor. "What do you mean?" he asked.

I stopped too, and grinned deeper. "He swapped DARTs; probably on purpose.

"The one he gave Sam was Duncan's. Which means it's a different technology, and who knows what it will lead to?"

As we reached the door to our new classroom, I added: "Oh yeah, and Sam says Duncan's bosses may well just want it back."

THE END

Pam Bloom was born in Liverpool, England, and now lives in nearby Meols, Wirral, with her husband, teenage daughter, cat and many, many fish. She has been writing since she was able to pick up a pencil, but this is her first completed novel. She hopes you enjoyed it – if you did, she would love you forever if you gave her a review, however short.

The second in the Parallel Universe Adventures, **Running**, will be published soon.

Connect with the author at
www.pambloomauthor.com -

Sign up for Pam's email list
and you will be sent FREE scifi reads

Don't miss out!

#0172 - 300117 - C0 - 175/108/11 - PB - DID1738572